First published in Great Britain in 2011 by Comma Press
www.commapress.co.uk

First published in Reykjavik as *Tvisvar á ævinni* by Skrudda, 2004.
Vera Júlíusdóttir's translation of the final story, 'The First Day of the Fourth
Week' first appeared in *Decapolis: Tales from Ten Cities* (Comma, 2006)

A CIP catalogue record of this book is available from the British Library.

ISBN   1905583362
ISBN-13   978 1905583362

LOTTERY FUNDED

The publisher gratefully acknowledges assistance from the Arts Council England
North West. With the support of the Culture Programme (2007-2013) of the
European Union.

Education and Culture DG

Culture Programme

Culture

This project has been funded with support from the European Commission.
This publication reflects the views only of the author, and the Commission
cannot be held responsible for any use which may be made of the information
contained therein. This book has been produced with the financial support of
Bókmenntasjóður, The Icelandic Literature Fund

Bókmenntasjóður
The Icelandic Literature Fund

Set in Bembo 11/13 by David Eckersall
Printed and bound in England by Short Run Press.

TWICE IN A LIFETIME

by
Ágúst Borgþór Sverrisson

Translated by
María Helga Guðmundsdóttir
& Anna Benassi*

*Second story translated by Vera Júlíusdóttir

Contents

Spilt Milk

WHO HAD THESE houses built? The merchants themselves,
the state, or the Iceland Dairy Cooperative? I mean the old
milk parlours and groceries, those little, unassuming stone
buildings, probably erected around 1950, indistinguishable
from other houses in the quiet streets of old neighbourhoods
except for one abnormally large and protruding bay
window. The milk parlour in this particular building stayed
in business until 1976, when it was converted into a private
residence, but the renovations were restricted to the interior
and the unaltered shop window became a strange living
room window.

A resident of the building, a man of about thirty,
vanished without trace in the summer of 1990 - got
separated from his friends at a club one Saturday night in
July and was never seen again. The friends said he had been
rather sombre and withdrawn that evening, and actually in
the preceding weeks as well, but this had neither caused
them to worry nor aroused their suspicion.

His car, a blue-grey 1988 Toyota Corolla, stood
untouched in front of the building for months after the
disappearance. Late that autumn, a photograph of the car
appeared in the tabloid *DV*, along with an article stating
that the man had neither been seen nor heard from, and that
his next of kin had not moved the car. The newspaper was
admonished for the article, which was considered insensitive
to the wife, for the story goes that she hadn't been able to
bring herself to touch the car after the man disappeared. Still,
many people doubted this story and asked why on Earth

the woman should eschew the car rather than the man's other possessions or their shared belongings. Those same people claimed that the woman had simply been depressed and listless after the event, as was to be expected, and hadn't moved the car for that reason. Others responded that she could hardly have been all that listless, since she moved out of the house shortly after the disappearance, and that this was why the abandoned vehicle had been considered newsworthy.

Public opinion was actually far more inconsiderate than the newspaper ever was: some said that the woman had cheated incessantly on her husband and that he had taken his own life in despair. Others asserted that she'd had him killed and that the car was somehow connected to the crime, though nobody could provide any reasonable explanation as to how that might have been.

The police didn't examine the car thoroughly, since the case was never treated as a criminal investigation. It was eventually sold late in 1991. Still today a shiver runs through me whenever I see cars like that out on the street. Yet I had nothing to do with the man's disappearance, except possibly as a small and invisible link in the chain of his destiny, and his vanishing is as much of a mystery to me as to others. I saw the Toyota in April of 1989, about a year before the man disappeared. The man himself I never laid eyes on except in photographs.

II

In the summer of 1971 I went regularly to the milk parlour for my mum. Outside the shop there was always a bright blue 1960 Ford Falcon. It was sparklingly clean and gleamed with polish at all times, not a speck of rust to be seen. It always stood there in the same place as if it were never used, like one of those cars that are no longer fit for driving and have even had their licence plates removed, though that was certainly not the case with this vehicle. Sometimes I immersed myself in a daydream where the car belonged to my dad: he had bought it that morning, stopped by the shop on his way home from work to buy milk and containers of skyr, the soft cheese that tasted delicious when Mum had stirred it together with cream, egg yolk, and a whole lot of sugar. A moment later Dad would pull up at home in the gleaming Falcon and invite me out for a ride while Mum would prepare dinner.

Dad had owned a pale blue 1955 Chevrolet. On Sundays we took a drive to the car dealerships and looked at new and used cars, only American ones: Mustang, Pontiac, Falcon, Chrysler.

I last saw the Chevrolet when it was hoisted aboard The Gullfoss in the autumn of 1969. Mum and I stood on the docks, but Dad was on deck and waved to us as the ship moved away. Gradually he shrank to a speck that disappeared. He was on his way to Australia by way of Denmark. Said that in Australia you could earn money and that when he came back he would buy a brand new ride.

He never went to Australia, however, nor did he come back home. For years he was in two minds as to whether he should continue south as he had intended or come back to Iceland, but for years and even decades he never knew which path to take and stayed in Denmark, the land he had looked upon as a rest stop, a temporary home.

One day when I was fiddling with the doorknobs on the Falcon I noticed that the lock-pins weren't down. I looked around: the street was deserted and silent. I opened the driver's door and sat down behind the wheel. I half expected the fresh smell of new seat leather, though I knew the car wasn't new. Instead it exuded an aroma of tobacco and aftershave. I didn't dare touch the gearshift or the accelerator, but turned the steering wheel and blew air through my lips, making engine noises. I inspected the dashboard: the speedometer showed miles instead of kilometres and only went up to 90. Just like it had in Dad's Chevrolet. At 60 miles per hour you were going quite fast, but I didn't know exactly how much that was in kilometres. I drove home and invited Dad and Mum for a ride. Mum said she was busy stirring skyr, but Dad came along and I drove us all around town. Dad thought the car was fantastic.

When I stepped out, the street was still empty and nobody was to be seen through the window of the milk parlour. But when I got home Mum stood in the front doorway, clenched fists at her hips, glaring at me. Someone had seen me through kitchen curtains and called her.

That night I dreamed of a beautiful woman who led me out of the house and along the neighbourhood streets. The woman said nothing, but in her face lived the promise of a wish fulfilled. The journey ended outside the milk parlour. There stood a car that looked exactly like the bright blue Falcon, except that it was pale blue like Dad's Chevrolet. On the inside it was a cross between the Chevrolet and the Falcon. For a brief instant I was filled with joy, but as soon as I touched the steering wheel my feelings turned to dread. I looked through a side window and saw myself standing inside the milk parlour. I was waving incessantly to myself from within, but the parlour began to retreat into the distance and turned into a passenger ship that sailed out into the ocean, gradually disappearing from view. I watched myself turn into a small speck.

I looked out the front window: the woman who had led me here stood in front of the car with her back turned. Though I couldn't see her, I could sense that she wasn't beautiful anymore. She had drawn a black hood over her head.

The next time Mum sent me to the milk parlour she made me promise not to touch any cars on my way, let alone take a seat in them. As usual, I was to buy three cartons of milk and one kilo of skyr. I put the goods in a green shopping net that I brought from home which I'd first laid eyes on long before I was old enough to go out to the milk shop.

When I turned away from the register with my purchases, I saw an old man walk up to the bright blue Falcon. I stopped in my tracks and stared out the window. He had stooped shoulders and a pot belly but seemed nonetheless to be in good shape, just like the car, light-footed, neat and dressed in athletic clothes, a short-sleeved shirt and pale trousers. He took a seat in the car, started the engine, and drove off.

As soon as the car vanished from sight, my faint hope was dashed. Dad had sent me a photograph of himself where he stood like an idiot in front of a red Fiat. In the letter he wrote: 'This is my new car. It's very fuel-efficient.' I had ignored this missive and convinced myself that Dad would soon enough be driving American wheels again. Now the damned red Fiat popped up in my mind again.

'What kind of oafishness is this,' said a harsh female voice next to me. I nearly jumped out of my skin. On the floor was a puddle of milk. I was so taken aback that I dropped the shopping net on the floor.

'The boy's thing is leaking,' said a man with a baseball cap. A moment later the girl from the register swooped down with a rag and new milk cartons. Her hair was almost white like the milk, but her cheeks grew pink from the exertion as she knelt on the floor with the rag.

III

One Friday night in April 1989 I was at a popular pub downtown. I had gone there against the wishes of my partner, who had slammed the front door after me with loud but empty threats to the effect that I shouldn't come back. We had been together for over three years, and now life in all its seriousness was before us: buying an apartment and having children in the near future. She had stopped partying and sat home on weekends instead, knitting children's clothes even though she wasn't pregnant, and reading the real estate section of *Morgunblaðið* even though we had no money. In contrast, I had spent the past several months preparing for this inescapable reality like a secondary school student faced with the start of a new academic year: I went out partying with friends every weekend. I knew it was wrong and didn't doubt my desire to commit any more than a teenager doubts that he wants to go to school though he may want to sleep late in the mornings. I was really just waiting for myself, waiting to lose interest in that kind of dissipation and nonsense.

On this particular evening, about the time when my friends had scattered about the pub while I alone remained seated at our table, something unusual if not exactly incredible happened: a rather attractive stranger sat down and struck up a conversation. I got the feeling that she was looking for something rather more than a conversation, even though I was quite average-looking, and the woman was neither heavily intoxicated nor did she seem in any way peculiar. I immediately became quite nervous and shy, as I was not particularly drunk, but I was also overcome with an irresistible, almost paralysing desire, not because I found the woman so attractive but simply as a result of getting such an opportunity on a silver platter. We chatted about varieties of beer, the music at the bar, and the South American novels that were so popular at the time. At the pub I often developed a passionate interest in multifarious issues and subject matters that, at other times, didn't matter to me in the least, and I couldn't possibly understand how I could have blathered for a whole evening and into the night about something I didn't give a damn about. Now I suddenly realised that we weren't really conversing – rather, I was expounding on and on while the woman interjected comments here and there in order to maintain something resembling a conversation. Sometimes she would try to catch my eye; usually I looked away out of shyness, but when I met her gaze she smiled invitingly.

When I became aware of the nature of the conversation I became tongue-tied and suddenly had nothing more to say about novels I hadn't read and beers that actually didn't taste at all different to me, especially not after I had downed four or five of them on a weekend pub crawl. At the very moment when the silence would have become awkward amidst the din of the pub, the woman told me, quite casually and apropos of nothing, that she lived in the West End, that her husband was out of town, and that they had no children. She suggested that we take a taxi back to her place right away.

I was living in a completely different neighbourhood by then and hadn't been to that street since I was a kid, but nevertheless it was familiar in the darkness. The moment I stepped out of the car I recognised the old milk parlour. I stared at the living room window, and for a moment I was pulled eighteen years back in time. The woman had stepped out of the car while I paid the fare, and she now stood by the door, fishing around for keys in a handbag. I felt like I'd been so humourless and nervous at the pub that I wanted to make up for it now, so I called out to her: 'You live in a milk shop. Your living room is an old shop window.'

She didn't answer, put a key in the lock and opened the door. It was then I noticed that she was wearing a hooded coat; she had drawn the black hood over her head.

★ ★ ★

She was suspiciously quick to fall asleep; perhaps she was giving me an opportunity to vanish without saying goodbye. I accepted it gratefully, hurrying to get dressed and leave the room. I felt a tingling sensation in my penis, but it was more like a fact in my mind than a genuine feeling: it was lacking that sated pleasure that requires a good conscience and relaxation. The woman had been in control in bed, bossy and on edge, and my experience had been more akin to a preview than real enjoyment of a new and strange female body.

I had taken off my shoes in the front hall, and though it was only rational to expect to see them lying there now, it still gave me a strange feeling, as shoes in a front hall are a sign that their owner either lives in the house or is a visitor there, not someone who steals in for a brief moment and then runs away. For reasons unknown this gave me a sense of calm. I put on the shoes, but instead of hurrying out I walked into the living room and looked out the old shop window.

The blackness was giving way to a pale blue pre-dawn half-light. The sleeping cars were dark like shadows. I inspected the living room. The floor had been tiled in a checkerboard pattern but I now stood on pale brown hardwood. Where the cash register had stood was now a green sofa. In the corner diagonally across from me was a TV set on a wheeled table. On the walls hung photographs in clip frames, among them a wedding picture. The bride in the photo must be the woman who was sleeping in the master bedroom, though I couldn't recognise her at all in the photograph, smiling ear to ear with ringlets in her hair.

Suddenly a white puddle of milk on the floor caught my eye. It vanished as quickly as it had appeared. I heard the echo of voices, but when I tried to listen it faded away and turned into the faint hum of a car motor or the buzzing of hot water pipes.

I looked back out the window, and there my eyes suddenly met with the bright blue Falcon! And what a sight it still was after all these years! It gleamed with polish, shining like a moon in the half-light.

I heard the sounds of someone waking up in the bedroom and hurried out into the still, cool air. I saw that the car wasn't a Falcon, but rather the car that the taxi had pulled up behind when we came here in the night – just an ordinary blue-grey Toyota Corolla, a new-looking car in good condition, but with splatters of mud on its sides.

I walked downtown and started looking around for a taxi, ready to face what I would meet at home, be it grave accusations or an unsuspecting woman fast asleep. When I approached midtown I began to hear raised voices, shouts of drunken revelry that sounded as if they were cheering for me and mocking me at once.

When I recall all this many years later I sometimes feel that the man must have disappeared just this night, especially if my mind wanders into this territory right before I fall asleep at night. But the man didn't go missing until over a year later. Once when I was in that grey area between semi-coherent thought and dreaming, I became convinced that he had met his fate at the very moment when the Falcon came back to haunt me through his living room window, my old milk shop window.

The First Day of the Fourth Week

9:30

THE TOILET MAT, a shaggy green rag, is meant to lie on the tiles next to the toilet base, curved into a semicircle which fits snugly to the base where it meets the floor. But the mat is never in its place; at best, it lies somewhere near to the toilet; at worst, in a bundle in a corner. Had he been asked a few weeks ago if there was a lavatory mat in his home, he would have been unable to answer that question. Now he recalls having seen the wife take this mat out of the washing machine and hang it up on a washing line. He might even have done it himself sometime, without giving any thought to what this was, this wet, green thing.

Why on Earth does a mat like this exist? Is it better that the pee which misses the bowl lands on a green mat so it becomes saturated with piss? His wife also scrubs the tiles every weekend; does she find that it is better to have to do both that and put the mat in the washing machine?

10:00

The heating. Geothermal heating doesn't bother you as long as you don't think about it. So far he has had other things to think about. But now as he finds himself at home in the middle of the day instead of coming home in the evening, his mind still on the job, now as he suddenly finds himself alone with himself in this house, the buzz of the

11

heating pipes suddenly starts to ring very loudly in his ears, reminding him that there are no radiators in the house, that the heating is in the walls. This came as a shock to him at the time they bought the townhouse, awoke in him a brief sense of insecurity, and then came the story of the accident which had once taken place in the house on the far end of the row. He had seen for himself the large moisture stain in the kitchen there.

He has not thought about this for many years. But what if one of the pipes bursts today? Tomorrow? A month from now? Sometime when you least expect it. Hot water flows into the concrete, causing it to crumble, in a short time the conditions will be like in a damp-ridden basement. The whole house might even be destroyed.

10:30

Did the kitchen tap start to drip before he lost his job or did he just not notice it before? He turns off both the hot and the cold water taps, tight. As tight as he can. But the dripping does not let up. There is a pipe wrench down in the storage room and he should be able to fix this, but the thought of attempting it and failing is more than his self-esteem can bear these days, so he decides not to. But the dripping grows constantly louder in his ears, accompanied by the buzzing of the heating pipes; this is the music to the image of the toilet mat in his mind.

11:00

How is he supposed to dress now? The wardrobe contains a collection of inexpensive suits, single jackets and trousers, shirts and ties. These are the work clothes he has put on daily, for years, without thinking, at random, almost without seeing what his hands pulled out of the wardrobe each time. But as he does not have any reason to visit an employment agency today, no reason even to pop into a bank, has no other reason to go out than to get out of the loud silence of the house, it does not seem appropriate to dress like he normally would; it would seem like a silly denial of the situation. And yet if he puts on jeans or a tracksuit, it is like a declaration that he has become inactive.

After a long deliberation he settles on a compromise, puts on a blue suit and a light blue shirt but leaves out the tie. He is pleased with his reflection in the mirror: the blue outfit is familiar and evokes a memory of normal days, the absence of a tie an appropriate acknowledgement of the change in situation.

12:00

He has always covered his back and already in the first week has managed to sell the 4x4, which came in handy as he is owed many months' salary. In the second week he contacted four employment agencies and applied for ten positions. In the third week he saw the employment agents again but the only news they had for him, each in their own words, was that these things took time.

Now the fourth week has begun and there is nothing to do except wait. Keep the mobile phone switched on when he is away from the house and check his email now and then.

4x4-less, he stands at the bus stop and waits there for a quarter of an hour. Finally a yellow bus arrives. Last time he travelled by bus, the buses were green. Back then they were also crammed with passengers, people on their way to and from work, students, elegant ladies. Sometimes the air on the buses was heavy with the smell of fish because of the fish factory workers, who have long since vanished from the city.

Now it is as if he steps into a less travelled parallel

reality: inside the bus are three East-Asian people, and a young man having a loud conversation with himself. He is wearing a torn denim jacket and his dirty hair sticks up into the air.

One more passenger joins the bus on the way: a very short man who trundles ahead of him three black plastic bags, packed with refundable containers. The bags stack up as high as the man's head and for the remainder of the journey he struggles to stay on his feet and to stop the bags from drifting around the bus. It is strange and almost fascinating to watch such a primitive fight for survival. The man does not look very elderly, for his body is too quick and firm. But his face is still covered in deep wrinkles. His skin is brown from dirt, not dark, but light brown, yet you can tell that this is not a suntan.

The smell coming off him is foreign and ambiguous, does not evoke repulsion, but rather a vague curiosity.

12:45

He has never been much of a café man, but has occasionally gone to one near his workplace on his lunch break when he has become bored with the cafeteria. Now he cannot think of any other place to go as he finds himself in the city centre for no reason. He feels like he is on a lunch break at work as he steps inside, but that feeling goes away quickly. Sitting at one table are civil servants whose faces he recognises, a woman and three men. The woman nods towards him. She has not greeted him before; he is stunned and reacts too slowly to return her greeting, and by then she has turned away, absorbed in conversation.

He orders the same as usual - a coffee and a bread roll with cheese. But he has no appetite now. He has not eaten anything today, does not want to admit to himself that he has lost all appetite, and silently curses himself for having ordered this, since he is not hungry and now the roll sits untouched on the plate like a symbol of some misery.

Four young builders in blue overalls are sitting at one of the tables, eating soup out of small bowls and nibbling at mini-slices of French baguette. This meal is as ill-suited to them as ballet dancing, those big and burly men of hard labour. But it is probably a sign of the times; the most unlikely people have begun to follow health tips, gulping down water all day long and eating light meals. And food has for some reason become much more fattening than it was a few decades ago. Back then men like this would have eaten a heavy lunch of meat, but would still have been thinner than these blokes.

After a while people go back to their jobs and the place empties, apart from a blind man who sits in a corner and talks to himself. This is the second man he encounters today who talks to himself. He wonders if there will be more before the day's out.

A good while later a chubby young man enters the café. His head is bowed, he is quite front-heavy and his movements are a bit sluggish, but a smile plays on his lips.

'I would like a large Danish pastry and cocoa with whipped cream, please,' he says to the waitress in a voice which could only be described as a loud whisper. 'It is my birthday today, you see,' he adds shyly when the food is on the table. The waitress does not respond to this but looks uneasy. This does not faze him and he says: 'I am 29 years old today,' and laughs. He then begins to talk to himself in that loud whisper and it is just as if he and the blind man in the corner are having a conversation.

He has another cup of coffee himself and continues to sit there, far too long. He reads the papers. One of them contains a news article on the liquidation, speculation that some money has been stashed away. He reads a few obituaries. He can not remember having done that before. They are extremely dull. He reads 'Readers' Letters'. A woman writes that she has seen men's shoes at a good price in Europris. A coat has been taken by mistake from a pub in Grafarvogur. An old man complains about communion wine he had drunk a year ago, that it tasted bitter. He hopes that this has been remedied.

He has a third cup of coffee. His stomach lets out loud gurgling sounds, not unlike the sound of a coffeemaker. The roll sits untouched on the white plate. He wonders how long it will take before it gets hard. It seems to him that the cheese slice has already begun to darken.

15:00

Why is he surprised? He knew better than this. What did he expect? Nonetheless it is a shock to him to see the empty and deserted company buildings. There is no sign of life here. For the last months they only worked on one floor in the old factory, and the cafeteria was still on the top floor of the newspaper building. Everything else was standing empty by then, but he paid no attention to it. There he sat, every day, and believed the repeated promises which now sound ridiculous.

The newspaper building has in fact stood empty for a whole year, ever since the paper was sold; the other companies went into liquidation. In this building he started his career more than 20 years ago and he once had a small office there on the top floor. Recently his advancement had been very rapid. As the other managers of the conglomerate fled in droves, he was constantly being promoted, to the point when he was second in charge to the owner, a man who had barely greeted him previously but was no longer the big entrepreneur he was before, because everything had shrunk.

In two buildings further south had been a small magazine publishing company, a radio station and a telemarketing business. All gone and the buildings empty.

In the old factory building was the other newspaper, the offices of its online counterpart, and an advertising agency. When the conglomerate began its operation in this building, there was talk that the factory belonged to an industry of the past and that now the future was moving into the building. The new factory, by contrast, is thriving; located at Grandi in the western part of the city, they do night shifts there and the machines are churning away 24 hours a day. Next to the old factory building was the print shop. It shut down two months ago.

The silence of the grave settles over him here. He has rarely felt such shame. He knows this is not his fault, but he was a part of it, believed the promises, stupidly worked at the same company for almost a quarter of a century and is now standing in the street, staring at the blank windows of buildings emptied of people.

Above all this seems unreal to him. Like in a stupid nightmare, the fact that he cannot enter the old factory building now, sit down at his desk and continue to work. Is it not actually more likely that he is sitting there now and is imagining this nonsense? That the person standing out here is a figment of the mind, his own imagination?

16:00

After a long, aimless but rather refreshing walk he goes into the bus station building. On light-brown lacquered wooden benches sit people who seem to be waiting for their luck to turn. Yet judging from their facial expressions, they have given up all hope but are still stubbornly waiting. Indistinct ages, coarse facial features, dirty hair and dirty clothes. The overall appearance shows the tell-tale signs of substance abuse, yet no one appears drunk or in an altered state at the moment.

He thinks to himself that at this time of day all the normal people are at work, but the weirdos hang out in cafés and bus station buildings and ride on the half-empty buses. Now he is with the weirdos.

He looks at his watch and it surprises and frightens him how time has flown. He has always been able to get a lot done quickly, and it is amazing to think how fast one can get used to doing nothing – time passes all the same.

For years he has moved through this area to go to the bank, or to a shop, or to fetch the car from a car park down here on the West Side when he could not find a spot up on the hill. Yet all this time he has never set foot in the bus station. And now when he finally comes in here, it is for no particular purpose, he who has never gone anywhere without a reason, never done anything without a purpose; although it now all seems to have been purposeless, all his toil throughout the years.

He decides to invent an errand by going to the gents', squeeze out a few drops and wash his hands.

He is shocked by his reflection in the mirror. In his expression he detects the shame he experienced earlier in the deserted work area, and the same hopelessness he detected in the expressions of the people on the wooden benches out in the waiting hall. His face seems dirty, the suit wrinkled and covered in stains, and there is also a spot on the shirt. It may be because of the peculiar light in here, how the lighting is reflected off the yellow walls. He did not look this bad in the mirror at home. For a moment it occurs to him that one always looks the way one feels.

17:45

They have not had a row since he lost his job. The memory of the constant arguments makes him nostalgic, it is a memory of security. Mainly they were about him being too absent-minded, and her having to be responsible for everything. He usually responded by listing the chores that he did. She said he did not do them properly and she had to organise all the work. He then said that he worked more than her and earned a higher salary. She said he was rarely at home and when he was at home his mind was always somewhere else.

Now there is not a cross word from her. No criticisms, nothing. She does not even ask him how the job search is going. She is silent and friendly. He fears that she will explode one day and there will be an almighty row.

Now the sink is filled with dirty dishes and the dishwasher is filled with clean ones. She asked him to do the kitchen this morning. Still sitting in the hall is the bag he was supposed to take down to the laundry room and empty into the machine. He forgot all this and now she has begun to prepare the meal in the dirty kitchen, having just arrived home from work; he has not lifted a finger all day. Never before has he been such an easy target, never has his cause been as hopeless, and therefore he feels as if a row has already started, although she does not say a word.

Despairing, he rushes to the bathroom and calls her from there. She emerges in the doorway, her face one big question mark.

'You, who's so perfect, why do you have this ridiculous mat here in the bathroom?' His voice shakes, he jerks his hand back and forth over the tiles and begins to ramble: '... piss mat... unhygienic... make-work... pointless...'

She answers calmly that it is only there for decorative purposes and points to an identically-coloured mat in the centre of the floor below the sink. He stares at this mat for a long time, has never noticed it before, but realises that it has been there for many years. And now, unusually, the toilet mat is level and straight, in its proper place. He looks from one mat to the other and now sees in them nothing but perfect harmony.

Defeated, he meets her glance but reads no victory in

her eyes; she is just worried. Softly she says that dinner will
be ready soon.

23:30

In bed, the day flashes through his head in disparate fragments:
a yellow bus, black plastic bags, deep wrinkles, a bread roll
on a white plate, blank windows in the old factory building,
a blue suit, a fat man eating a Danish pastry, bad communion
wine, small soup bowls, blue overalls, the dripping from
the kitchen tap, the woman from the ministry's nod, cheap
men's shoes, a blind man talking to himself. The day is a
collection of pointless and sad details and he feels there is no
unity in the world anymore.

But then he tries to think about the mats in the
bathroom again, a green mat by the toilet base, a green mat
beneath the sink, and he senses the harmony, a perfect green
harmony and the green colour spreads across his mind's eye,
turning into a meadow stretching out further than the eye
can see.

He can feel her hand on his. He hesitates, then he
squeezes her hand and she squeezes his in return. As he drifts
off into sleep he feels her speaking to him in a soothing
voice: reassuring words. But it is only a dream. She is inside
her own dream, tossing and turning in the dark.

Translated from the Icelandic
by Vera Júlíusdóttir

The German Teacher's Wife

WHEN JÓHANN WENT broke in Germany, he often thought of the jar of spare change in his bedroom back home. The summer before, he had gotten into the habit of stowing his small change there when he was loaded and wanted to lighten his wallet and pockets. But by the last week of every month he was broke, and then he emptied the jar. Its contents were often a pleasant surprise; they could be unexpectedly ample, enough for a pack of cigarettes and a cinema ticket. Once he was able to go out and party with the contents of the jar and a hundred krónur he found under a couch cushion: cover charge plus three vodka-and-waters plus a taxi.

In mid-July he had taken a girl out to dinner with the jar money and what he got for the empty bottles accumulating in plastic bags in the basement. This was before the centralisation of the recycling service, so he took all the plastic bags to a grocery shop. The girl at the cash register, who was tasked with counting the bottles with him, was not at all pleased. The air in the back room grew saturated with the smell from the bags, at once sweet and rotten. They chatted while they placed the bottles in empty wooden and plastic crates, and the girl's mood gradually lightened. He found her quite cute, which prompted the realisation that he had no desire to take the other girl out to dinner. The latter's name was Sigrún, and he had met her at Óðal a couple of weeks ago, where she had stared at him for a long while and then practically ordered him to sit down and talk to her. He rather had the feeling that she had ordered him to take her out to dinner tonight as well, although on the surface

21

of it she had only hinted at it rather aggressively. The shop girl smiled at him when the transaction was completed and looked as if she were waiting for him to say something. He stood nervously in front of her for a moment but then left without saying goodbye.

That evening he expounded upon his plans to Sigrún over steak and red wine at Askur. He was going to spend one semester in Germany, then come home and enrol at the University of Iceland next fall. While overseas he was going to build a solid foundation in the language, but mostly he was just going to enjoy living abroad for a while, free and independent. If he got a minimum grade on an enrolment exam in German, he would be placed on a course for foreigners and could get student loans. After the course was completed, he would take a second enrolment exam in German and would need to pass that to get more student loans. But instead of enrolling at that university he would come home and go to UI.

'I like the sound of that,' said Sigrún. 'I agree to it, for my part.'

Jóhann's eyes opened wide in shock. He thought she was joking, but she hadn't cracked a joke in the two weeks he had known her. She continued and said it would surely be difficult to be without him for such a long time, but this was a sensible decision and she wasn't one to object to sensible decisions. And who knew? She might even be able to visit him. He stared at her, speechless. She seemed to misunderstand his gaze, blushed, smiled shyly and averted her eyes, looking down at the plate, the half-eaten piece of meat, and the potato peel in its foil wrapper.

He thought to himself that he had better set things straight right away, but he hesitated, didn't want to spoil the evening by causing a scene in a restaurant. Besides, he didn't mind the thought of sleeping with her tonight even though he would rather do it with someone else. She had short red hair, a pale complexion, and not too many freckles.

She was a bit on the thin side for his taste and almost flat-chested. Her green eyes were lovely, but her voice was loud and unpleasantly sharp and her face bore some intangible expression of harshness that robbed her of charm. The girl in the shop had been buxom and curvaceous, with lush lips and long wavy hair that shimmered and a face that lit up when she smiled. When Sigrún smiled, she tightened her thin lips as if trying to keep the smile under wraps.

He hadn't copped off in a month. He felt as if he could get any woman he wanted every time he stepped into Óðal, marching like a cowboy through wooden saloon doors, part of the interior design that had been adopted for a screening of the John Travolta film *Urban Cowboy*. But the film had flopped and nobody knew anymore why the place was furnished this way, since there wasn't a cowboy hat in sight and the newest pop songs were played on the dance floor, not a hint of country music. His trawling hadn't borne fruit in a long time, though, and Sigrún had spoiled everything these last few weeks.

They went back to her place around midnight. She dragged him into the bedroom and began unbuttoning her blouse. She steered him on top of her and under her, prevented him from trying anything perverse. Once, when he brought his penis to her lips, she said: 'Are you crazy!'

She insisted on keeping the lights out. He was relieved.

At his graduation celebrations, he had experienced ecstasy and the promise of more ecstasy. Now he would never have to set foot in secondary school again, and the future was one big summer party. When he thought back to graduation, he felt that it had been either yesterday or many years ago; it defied his perception of time. His mother had asked him whether he was planning on throwing a party, whether he could afford something like that. He jumped, hesitated, and then answered that he didn't want any party. The fatigue in her face flowed into him and became his guilt.

She had raised two children on her own, and everything in her expression seemed to indicate that she wouldn't live long enough to regain her strength from that ordeal. Last winter she had met a man who worked the graveyard shift and slept all day in her bed while she was at work. But in the evenings they sometimes roused themselves and went into the living room, poured themselves a drink, looked at photographs, and chatted about their genealogies. Jóhann never sat with them. He'd felt like a paying guest in the household since the man moved in. His father had sent congratulations via telegram from the United States on his graduation day. Jóhann was glad he hadn't come, because they were always shy and awkward around each other.

Now the weeks raced by and each day was like an instant in time. Suddenly August was half over and the voyage to Germany was only just over a month away. Anxiety and excitement preyed on his mind. He looked forward to new adventures, but no money was accumulating besides the change in the jar that he emptied every month. He wouldn't get the student loan until after the enrollment exam, so he would have to do better if he planned to cover airfare, rent, and food for the 2-3 weeks before the exam. He worked 50 hours a week in a warehouse, but weekends ate up his pay and the car guzzled petrol. He also smoked a pack a day, more on weekends.

Sigrún didn't try to crash the all-male parties that Jóhann and his friends held every weekend, but she was usually there at Óðal by the time they appeared there, having spent the whole evening arguing about what music they should play and snatching each other's records off the turntable without allowing a single song to play through to the end. Every day he intended to break the relationship off, but he always put it off. The thought of confrontation made him anxious, and there was something else holding him back as well, a vague feeling that called the change jar in his bedroom to mind, though he had no idea what the jar could have to do with it. Once he dreamed that he had broken up with Sigrún. She took it with incredible equanimity, but the jar fell to the floor and shattered.

The entrance exam was around mid-October, his employment ended in early September, and he was planning to leave just before the end of the month. But as September wore on he found himself broke once again; couldn't even afford the fare. Sigrún had all of her savings, hundreds of thousands, and most of her summer earnings. She offered to lend him 50 thousand. He refused unconvincingly. She said it was far more sensible for him to borrow from her without interest than to take a wickedly expensive bank loan. She also encouraged him to quit smoking and calculated how much money it would save him in six months. He asked whether she thought she knew what cigarettes cost in Germany. She asked whether he thought they were free out there.

He sold his car for 20 thousand, which he added to the 50 thousand from Sigrún. When he recalls this now, he has no sense of how much 70 thousand krónur was worth in 1983. This was two years after the currency change; 50 krónur had gone pretty far back in 1981, but runaway inflation was warping his memory now as much as it had distorted all sense of price back then. Still, he feels that a red five-hundreder gave you as good a feeling in the fall of 1983 as the two-thousander with Kjarval on it does now.

He does recall very clearly, however, that the money didn't last long in Germany. The first weeks were full of ecstatic freedom and novelty: trains, elaborate Gothic buildings, crowded streets, pubs on every corner, glorious German beer, restaurants, discos. There was certainly no shortage of beautiful girls at the discos, but his weak German made him nervous. He decided to boost his self-confidence by sprucing up his wardrobe, and bought three brightly coloured suits, three Hawaiian shirts, two white shirts and a black leather tie. He turned up the cuffs on his suit jackets and popped his unbuttoned collar, and sometimes he let the leather tie dangle untied around his neck. He started talking more to the ladies in German with a sprinkling of English thrown in, or German-infused English, depending on how good he was feeling about himself. But they were unimpressed and he reaped no rewards for his efforts, except for one time when he wound up very drunkenly snogging a girl outside a club. He couldn't remember what the girl looked like, but her friend had stood to one side and hurried her on.

He was relieved to be rid of Sigrún. Now the relationship would die of natural causes. If she tried to make good on her intentions of visiting him, he would dump her in a letter. When he went to bed at night, he sometimes thought about his German teacher from last winter. He was a chap of around forty, not particularly lame or boring per se but also not in the least interesting, no more than any other teacher. He always had a rather ugly tie on and wore a tank-top. He also had a bald spot, though to be fair, he didn't make a bad thing worse with a comb-over.

Jóhann had got 75% in his diploma exam in German, which was his highest grade. His lowest was 45% in maths, and his average was just under 65%. He had no particular interest in German, or any other subject for that matter, but it seemed logical to him to choose what he was best at. He hadn't thought at all about it before he left for Germany, but now he found himself thinking that if his plans succeeded he would probably end up teaching German in secondary school. He hadn't set himself any real goals other than finding some place to belong in life, but this must be the likeliest result. It was a strange feeling, though, to envision himself as a teacher in a few years. He refused to believe it would make him seem like a geek; he was determined never to be geeky, not in five years, not in twenty. He wouldn't wear tank-tops but well tailored and smart-looking clothes. Either he would have a fabulous-looking wife, maybe a blonde fashion model, or he'd be single. He actually liked the sound of the latter option better. He could keep going to Óðal, since he couldn't imagine that such a popular place would ever close. Maybe he would go to Óðal and Hollywood by turns, run into his students there, and maybe even dance with the girls who'd think to themselves that they'd never met such a cool teacher before.

The money was gone almost before he realised he was broke. The day he took the placement exam he had five marks left, a silver hunk that for some reason reminded him of the commemorative coin from the 1974 National Festival; this coin was considerably smaller, though. He had breakfast at a café in the university district and went to the exam with just over two marks in his pocket. Results were posted the same day, and he was placed on the second-lowest level course for foreigners. He got a stamped form from the office and sent it along with a handwritten letter back to the Student Loan Office.

He couldn't expect to receive any money for at least ten days, maybe two weeks. He went into a grocery shop, turned the small change over in the palm of his hand and looked at price labels. After some searching he found a piece of cheese and a sausage package that together cost five pfennig less than what he had left. The sausage package contained only one large multicoloured sausage, which he was afraid might be spicy, but on his tongue it was reminiscent of unusually flavourless haggis. It almost crumbled in his mouth. He hadn't eaten food this bad since he had arrived here, maybe not for as long as he could remember.

His rented room was half an hour's walk or five minutes by train away from the university district. He ate half of the cheese and the sausage in his room, without cutlery or a plate, and put the rest on the windowsill. He stared out the window. The windows in the house across from him were decorated with elaborate lion images; the silent lions gaped at him. Still, it was only a rental building with flats and single rooms housing labourers, taxi drivers, and students.

Here everything was tall and decorative – no patchwork corrugated iron roofing.

The windowsill was sooty. He drew a finger through the soot. This was foreign dirt; he could sense the difference without being able to put his finger on it. It was an empty and cold foreign windowsill; here there was no change jar half-full of silver-grey marks with gold pfennigs on the bottom.

He had hardly spent any time in the room these first weeks – only while he slept – and so it hadn't bothered him how bare and uninviting it was. Now he had nowhere else to go, nothing to disappear off to. The floorboards were covered in patches of hardened glue, because the previous tenant had ripped up the carpet and taken it away with him. There were no pictures on the walls. No curtains. His landlord had procured a mattress that lay on the floor, and the only furniture was an old desk and a tired-looking chair with a dark red upholstered seat; both had come with the room. He left his clothes in a heap at the foot of the mattress. He tended to his hygiene in a bathroom down the hall, which he shared with other tenants he never saw.

Over the next few days, he found himself in a different and drearier world than the city had presented to him thus far. He had gone from small city to big city to small, empty room. He starved himself every other day, but on the intervening days he went out to the grocery shop wearing multi-pocket jeans and stuck a block of cheese and a sausage in each side pocket. He always took the same kind of cheese and the same multicoloured sausage; something told him that if he deviated from this pattern he would get caught.

Fortunately the course wasn't supposed to start until the end of the month. He tried to shorten the wait for the money by sleeping as much as possible. He woke up at all hours of the day and night, and often he would go back to sleep without having the faintest notion what time it was, except that sometimes it was light outside and sometimes dark. He often thought he was at home in Iceland when he woke up, and this sensation was often connected with what he had just been dreaming. Once he thought he had just taken a nap on the living room sofa while his mother sat in the kitchen and smoked; another time he thought he was too late for work and jumped out of bed, only to be faced not with an Icelandic summer morning but an empty and pointless German afternoon in a world where everyone but him seemed to have a purpose.

He also thought about killing time by writing some letters that he could send later. He didn't intend to write to Sigrún – that didn't seem sensible – and yet it hung over him like an unpleasant duty that he meant to neglect all the same. He wanted to write to his friends but knew that they would never be bothered to reply. They were fine friends, but if he knew them as well as he knew himself he could be sure that they hardly thought of him nowadays, even though they would surely welcome him back with open arms when he returned home, ready to party.

Most of all he wanted to write to his mother, though he couldn't understand why. The hunger and the loneliness awakened in him a vague but insistent desire for her to be more nosy, that she write to him incessantly and call him with unnecessary worries.

He wrote her a single page. Didn't mention lack of funds once, but described the university buildings and the cathedral downtown, said the exam had gone well, the German beer was good, the subway was overfull sometimes. At the bottom of the page he signed off, 'With warm regards, Jóhann.'

The following day a letter arrived from Sigrún. It was written with a green Bic pen. The handwriting was very clear, the letters even and straight. She was scandalised by a friend who had snogged a stranger on the dance floor. Said she had a hard time talking to her since then. She hoped that the money was lasting well, as indeed it should. She asked whether he had quit smoking. He grinned. He hadn't smoked recently because he was so broke. He had actually lit up an old butt the other day and taken a deep drag on it, then found another butt, but after that he ran out of matches.

'And of course you've stopped getting drunk,' Sigrún wrote. He should eat in the cafeteria at the university and cook at home, not waste money at restaurants. She thought it would be okay if he had a beer from time to time, but he should buy it in a shop, not gulp it down in bars. She wrote disapprovingly of his friends, whom she sometimes saw around town or out partying, though it wasn't clear exactly what it was that offended her about them. There was just a general snort of disdain in the green letters on the line-ruled paper.

She ended her letter with the following words: 'Anyway, I just hope you're doing as well as possible, your Sigrún.' The last words were heartfelt by her standards, and he had never said anything kinder than this to her. He sensed - or thought he sensed - what she had been thinking when she wrote this, saw her face in his mind, the look she gave him sometimes and then looked away when he met her eyes.

He laid the letter aside, sat down on the mattress, sighed, and thought of nothing at all for a moment. Suddenly he felt an outburst of irritation that resembled an idea or a discovery. Why was she playing this game? She knew full well that he wouldn't stop smoking, drinking, or spending money. She was no fool, for all her stubbornness. Why then all this pretence? Since she couldn't leave him in peace, then why didn't she write him something other than advice that she knew he would never follow?

He decided to keep the letter out of a sort of gratitude to her. He folded the pages and picked up the envelope. It was addressed with the same green pen. The address was incorrectly spelt, but there was only one letter's difference in the street name. When he was about to put the pages

30

back in the envelope he discovered that it wasn't empty. He pulled out another green-lettered sheet. It bore the following message: 'I know all sorts of things can come up when people are abroad, and it's also just good policy to have some back-up funds. I recommend that you put this in a good bank account. Can't you get excellent interest over there?' He felt around inside the envelope again and pulled out yet another sheet of paper, but this one wasn't covered in green writing; it was typewritten. It was a cheque made out to him for five hundred German marks.

The One Who Isn't There

KRISTÍN AWOKE TO the sound of the letterbox snapping shut. She had a mental image of bills, flyers, and other things of no interest to her falling on the floor of the front hall. The thought brought with it a feeling of emptiness. When she woke again, it was well after one in the afternoon. Occasionally she overslept, and was too late even for her evening shift, which started at four o'clock.

When Kristín got up she had completely forgotten the snap of the letterbox, but the door into the front hall was open and her glance fell on a small card that lay on the floor by the front door. She went into the hall and picked it up without much interest.

It was a postcard addressed to her. But she couldn't make head nor tail of it, and she didn't know the sender. The man was on a beach holiday in Portugal with his family, but in spite of this pleasant setting he couldn't get her out of his mind. 'I long for you,' he had written. She felt warm all of a sudden, an electric current surged through her body, and her heartbeat grew loud and fast.

But it didn't make any sense. For one moment she tried to believe that she had a secret admirer. But that was impossible. It was obvious that the man knew the woman he was writing to. This remained a mystery for a short while, but the answer was staring her in the face: the card wasn't meant for her. It was addressed to Kristín E. Sigurðardóttir, which was indeed her name, but the address was completely different. The street wasn't even in the neighbourhood, though it was actually close to the shop where Kristín worked.

She got over her disappointment quickly, because now she had a different mystery on her hands: who was this woman? Who was this person who shared her name and was the object of a married man's desires? She must have seen her in the shop at some point, since she'd worked there for two straight years, after school during winters and full-time in summer.

She tried to call the customers' faces to mind but was suddenly gripped with an incomprehensible hunch that the woman wasn't among them, and her mind went as empty as a blank screen: she couldn't remember a single face. She wondered whether she was even awake yet. This was a lot like the dream she often had before waking. She ran her fingers over the card, read it again, and convinced herself that this was reality.

She put the postcard in the brown hippie-esque shoulder bag that was hanging on the same hook as the pale blue denim jacket. She had worn this jacket and the feather-light bag all summer long. Once upon a time both had been brand new, fresh and tempting, each in its own shop. Those had been two lovely days when she bought them, the day of the brand new denim jacket and the day of the new shoulder bag. Now both items had become humdrum and dull.

The summer had been an uneventful one. It'd been switched off like a lightbulb that had glowed brightly in the spring. In the first two weekends after school ended, she'd been to two memorable parties. At the first one she walked in on her friend Svandís, at it with two guys. They didn't seem to notice her. She was so surprised that rather than bolting immediately she watched their play for a few moments before closing the door again.

She slipped away from the party, suddenly quite sober, with a dry mouth, burning cheeks and feeling tingly all over. She hadn't fucked in a long time, actually only three times in her life. For the rest of the week she couldn't shake the image of three naked bodies from her mind.

Two weeks later she wound up snogging a boy she had never seen before. He was a gentle sort with delicate features, and she kept admiring his face and clamping it between her palms like the head of a cute puppy. It was lovely to forget herself unashamedly in the pleasure of it. She was drunk that night and they drifted apart in the crowd; she couldn't find him again. It was like the kind of dream where you wait for something to happen and wake up before it does.

She was left with nothing but a sweet memory, neither a name nor a phone number. She didn't dare ask about him; the mere thought of discussing boys was terrifying. She didn't expect to meet him soon, but she never saw him again, not at parties, not on the street, nor in cafés. Nothing happened at subsequent parties, nobody paid her any attention; she was never properly drunk and always felt uncomfortable. Svandís and Linda were lost in their boy-chasing. The party-going died down in mid-June.

The girls gradually stopped getting in touch. Linda responded coldly when Kristín visited her one day at the bakery where she worked. She herself stopped making contact and hadn't heard from them since early July.

She worked the evening shift every weekday and every other weekend. At midnight, when she came home from work, she thought it was dinnertime. Noon had become early morning. She always felt she was sleeping too much, and sleep made her drowsy. From when she woke up until the start of her shift was the longest part of the day, except on those days when she overslept.

It was nearly impossible to make clotted time flow again. She couldn't convince herself to do anything but wait. She had no appetite at all, but then ate too much at the shop at night. Earlier this summer she had occasionally dropped by a café downtown, in the hope that someone might check her out or talk to her. But nothing happened and no-one seemed to notice her; she might as well have been invisible. The boy at the party last spring had become like any other daydream.

She heard the whoosh of the bus as it drove up the next street. Strange how often she ended up being late for her shift even though she was dying of boredom from the moment she woke up. If she didn't want to show up late, she would have to get a taxi. That wasn't a problem in itself. She had hardly spent any money recently, and though the pay was quite low, she had tens of thousands in her bank account and a handful of notes in her wallet.

She thought of her car, a 1992 Mazda. She had bought it a year ago. It'd broken down three weeks later, and the repairs cost more than the car had. Five months later it broke down again. This time she asked her father to repair it, which he did, but said again and again that Njörður wasn't too good to do this sort of thing. He never called him Njörður, only repeated the phrase 'your stepfather' in a voice loaded with mockery and bitterness, as if he laid some of the blame for his own marital history at her door. It had never occurred to her to think of Njörður as her stepfather, and nobody expected as much of her. He was an expressionless and indifferent man who left her completely alone.

The car had broken down for the third time in mid-July and had stood untouched on the street since then. She was always about to take it to a mechanic, but for the most part she tried to pretend it didn't exist.

It must have been quite a while, actually, since she had looked at the car, because it now appeared that it had turned into a heap of rust. She stiffened. Moved closer. The license plates had been removed. She had a strange feeling of horror. Through the windows she could see strange twists of metal, and the back seat had vanished.

She glanced a few metres further west and saw where her car actually stood. Same make, same colour, less rust. She walked over there and observed that nothing had changed. It looked quite all right, just wouldn't start up the last time she tried. A brown paper bag lay in the driver's seat. She didn't remember what was in it. Something or other that she had bought when she drove it last. She didn't want to know what it was.

Climbing into the taxi evoked a strange feeling. The last time she had taken a taxi was in June, on the way home from a party on a bright summer night. The face of the boy she had kissed last spring appeared in her mind, clearer than before, almost tangible. Still, it was as if he hadn't existed, was only a figment of her imagination.

She had a break at 7 o'clock and decided to use it to return the misdirected postcard. She would have preferred to put it in an envelope so the recipient wouldn't suspect that she'd read it and the encounter would be less uncomfortable. But she couldn't find an envelope in the shop. She slipped the card into a green plastic bag of the type usually used for sweets; the coloured plastic nearly covered the writing, and she hoped that the woman wouldn't take the card out of the bag before she said goodbye. Nonetheless she looked forward to seeing this woman, finding out who she was.

The house was about two minutes' walking distance from the shop. On the way she thought about the man who had looked her in the eyes today and smiled at her. When she handed him his change his fingers had lingered on her palm for an unnecessarily long time. She blushed. She couldn't remember when a man had last paid her any attention. This one was almost certainly over forty and not handsome, albeit well-dressed; he was far too red in the face. Still, the incident had given her an unexpected tingle of excitement. She was touched by the man's desire, not the man himself; the fact that desire was directed at her. She remembered how disgusted she had been in the past when men of that age stared at her in bars.

The house was greyish-brown with a red roof; basement, main floor, and attic. She walked up the steps and read the doorbells. They were labelled, but she couldn't find the name on them. She checked the basement. The doorbell was unlabelled and she rang it. A sleepy young man in his early twenties opened the door. She couldn't tell whether he had just woken up or simply had a drowsy-looking face. His attire contrasted sharply with his expression: fine black trousers with creased cuffs, a nice belt and an unlabelled black t-shirt. He wore black shoes, polished to a shine. The boy didn't recognise the name Kristín E. Sigurðardóttir, but confessed that he had no idea who his neighbours were.

She walked back up the stairs and rang the labelled doorbell. There was no response on the main floor, but the door to the attic apartment opened and a woman appeared, a regular at the shop; she had worked there for a while and sometimes still made herself at home behind the register. The woman burst out laughing when Kristín announced her errand.

'Kristín Sigurðardóttir - isn't that you?' The woman didn't seem to have any interest in the reason for this oddity. She was just mightily amused and glowed with the delight of someone who always has an open mind towards anything strange and funny without reflecting on it any further. Kristín tried to explain herself but became tongue-tied, her words were hesitant and disjointed, and the woman laughed louder and louder until Kristín turned tail and fled. The woman called after her to send her best to everyone at the shop.

When she came home around midnight, Njörður was sitting in the living room, watching TV. She couldn't see his face, and he didn't seem to notice her. She looked at the back of his head: his messy dirty-blond hair and bald spot. He rested his feet on a footstool. Dark socks. He never seemed to wear slippers and his feet always emitted a faint, sour odour that mingled with the house smells until it escaped notice. It occurred to Kristín that it might just as well have been her father sitting in the armchair and watching TV. It wouldn't have made the least bit of difference. He had done as much for years on end, watched TV in the living room in the evenings and not spoken to her, neither in conflict nor in friendship. When she was little it was different; then she sometimes sat in his lap and watched *Dallas* with him.

For no apparent reason she tiptoed into the living room instead of heading straight for her bedroom as planned. Njörður was fast asleep. He had a younger-looking face than the back of his head would suggest; the messy hair and the bald spot. On TV was the actor John Thaw in a courtroom, wearing a white wig. He rose to his feet and addressed the judge. The volume was turned down. The smell of feet hung in the air, faint but present.

She had first seen Njörður two years ago at the café Kaffisetrið, near the bus depot at Hlemmur, where she occasionally stopped after school, sipped soft drinks and leafed through her textbooks, sometimes alone, sometimes with Svandís. Njörður, who then was a nameless stranger, always sat there alone, smoking and skimming through the newspapers with nervous movements and a facial expression that suggested that he was looking for something terrible about himself in the papers. She could never have imagined that her mother would start seeing this same man a few months later. The future could be unpredictable, after all.

She walked past their open bedroom: her mother was fast asleep, too. The lamp on the bedside table was still on. She went into her bedroom and sat down by the desk that she had been given as a confirmation present four years ago.

She laid the postcard on the table. Was going to look at it again, but suddenly the mystery didn't evoke excitement anymore, just boredom and a sense of fatigue. Still she tried to think up a possible explanation - this woman must be somewhere, she thought - but couldn't get any farther. Her mind was suddenly filled with a thought about the future, unclear at first but then remarkably clear. They weren't reflections about her own future, about what lay ahead - not a bit of that - but about the nature of the future, always unpredictable but still so logical when it became the present and you thought everyone should have been able to see it coming.

She was usually wide awake at this hour of the night,

but the feeling of emptiness, her fatigue over the riddle, made her sleepy and her thoughts became dreamlike even though she was sitting in a chair and holding her head in her hands. Suddenly she was gripped by something that had been love but had turned into obsession. The feeling was at once completely strange and familiar. There was a man on the phone. He was drunk, affectionate and drunk. He said he had been sunbathing all day and had thought of nothing but her. He felt she was the burning hot sun. He said he had fallen asleep and dreamed of her. He slurred his words. He said: 'I'll never forget the first time I saw you in the shop.'

Exchange of Guilt

THE STORY OF the good brother and the bad brother exists in countless variations, both in literature and in life. Still, it is often not so much about good and evil as it is about an unfortunate brother and a fortunate one. Ólafur often thought about this, but he drew a blank if he tried to conjure up the specifics of different versions. He remembered Cain and Abel from the Bible stories he read in primary school but had forgotten who killed whom. He had a vague recollection of the mini-series *Rich Man, Poor Man* from the seventies, with Nick Nolte and Peter Strauss playing the Jordache brothers. Thinking of the series awakened in him a critical feeling towards the brother story, although he could hardly remember anything from the show, just an unclear mental image of some villain called Falconetti who was neither of the brothers.

Above all, Ólafur was living just such a story. He and Oddur were the two brothers made flesh: Ólafur the CEO of a respected company, married with two children, while Oddur was divorced, unemployed and bankrupt, had been convicted of fraud, and was sometimes drunk in public.

During the boys' youth, their father ran an auto workshop behind their home. Once Oddur stole some money from the company's cash register. He threw his friends a little party with goodies from the local shop with part of the stolen money, but returned what was left when he was found out. The father, who usually didn't hold back when scolding Oddur, didn't take it too badly, but still made him work without pay until the debt was repaid. The father thus seemed to know exactly how much money was in the register at any time, and so it came as a shock to Oddur a few months later to be accused of stealing a second time. This time he protested his innocence vehemently. But the father was so certain of his case that for a time even Oddur doubted his own innocence. And this time there was no mercy, even though he was innocent. The father gave him a scathing dressing-down, said he could never trust him again, that he would certainly grow up to be a criminal later in life.

As it happened, Ólafur was the one who had taken the money. He had done it in childish innocence; it hadn't really been a theft. He was seven years old and didn't really understand the nature of money yet. But he had a lot of fake money and routinely cut sheets of paper into strips, then notes which he wrote and drew on with markers. These he kept in an old Mackintosh toffee tin. One evening he took a few bills from the cash register and added them to the stack in the Mackintosh tin. After he heard father accuse Oddur of the theft, he took the tin down to the beach and buried it near the water's edge.

Ólafur never fully revisited this childhood memory, but every time he cheated on Steinunn, his wife, the Mackintosh tin came to mind.

At the father's wake, the brothers had plans to meet soon and chat together, raise a glass and trade memories about the old man. 'Stop by for a visit one evening,' said Ólafur. 'Steinunn and the kids would be glad to see you.' - 'You bet I'll be there,' said Oddur, misty-eyed and nodding vigorously as if such a visit would be a remarkable achievement. Ólafur thought to himself that in his constant attempts to turn over a new leaf, Oddur had probably grown accustomed to praise for deeds that were normal and unremarkable for other people. He had cried at the funeral, which made Ólafur feel rather like an outsider, as the father's death didn't make much of an impact on him. The father and Oddur had been much closer, even though the father lambasted Oddur constantly but never said a single critical word to Ólafur or about him.

One evening, about two weeks after the funeral, Oddur called. He was at a pub in Kópavogur and made no mention of calling round. 'Weren't we going to have a pint together?' he asked in a familiar whining voice, as if Ólafur were already late to a planned date.

Ólafur had never been to this place before. Near-darkness greeted him, dark wood and a large pot belly in a tight, light grey t-shirt. The owner of the belly stood with his back to the bar and stared at Ólafur; he had a pint in his outstretched hand and sniggered.

Ólafur looked around and spotted Oddur in a small group in the corner. Oddur waved to him and crowed, not without a hint of the familiar whine: 'Oi, aren't you treating your big brother to a drink?'

Ólafur ordered two beers at the bar. The man with the grey belly inspected him surreptitiously and nodded vigorously when their eyes met for a moment, snapped his fingers and said, 'Baugur[1] News, goddamn capitalist Baugur News and conservative media mafia.' The snigger turned into a loud laugh and the belly shook.

The group in the corner were a good deal more appealing. Two young girls – one fat with a kindly expression, the other pretty with long, blond hair – sat and talked to a strong-featured man in his fifties. Oddur sat cheerfully next to the man, but stood up when Ólafur approached with the beers and directed him to a booth nearby.

The man with the strong features was reminiscing in a hoarse voice about his career in the music industry in the seventies. The girls listened attentively but contributed little

1. An Icelandic investment company that made numerous investments in British industry and filed for bankruptcy in the wake of the 2008 financial crisis. The company became emblematic of unrestrained free-market capitalism in Iceland, and also owned Iceland's largest newspaper — referred to disparagingly by politicians as 'Baugur News'.

to the discussion. There were no other guests apart from a young man who seemed to be using the place as an office, sat alone at a table with a laptop in front of him and stacks of paper and notebooks to the side. His long hair was pulled back in a ponytail.

The grey belly kept giggling at the bar.

'Hey, it's great to see you, man,' said Oddur, who sounded a little nervous and had his eyes open wide. Often every shade of emotion seemed to well up in him at once, making it hard to tell them apart. Now he added sarcastically, 'Yeah, you don't meet much in the way of fancy people nowadays.' The mocking tone was laced with admiration. Ólafur recognised all of this and remained unfazed.

'Cheers to the old man,' said Oddur and raised his glass. Ólafur joined his toast. Oddur started reminiscing about the father, and it seemed to Ólafur that tears came to his eyes. He felt a bit like a bereavement counsellor. Oddur's stories became rather convoluted and disjointed, and Ólafur began glancing at the people in the corner when not contributing nods and monosyllables.

The girls were still listening to the ex-musician. Suddenly the blonde met Ólafur's gaze, smiled, and looked away.

He had cheated on Steinunn exactly five times with as many women. He hadn't seen any of them again. The remarkable thing was that he had never been rejected. Five attempts, five one-night stands. He was certainly a fairly handsome man, but he harboured no illusions about being irresistible. But it was almost as if he had some insight that allowed him to recognise which women were willing and when. Unless, of course, it had all been pure luck.

'...maybe it isn't right to dig this up when the poor old man is still warm in his grave...' The blonde girl smiled at him again and looked at him for so long that he had to look away this time. He was losing the ability to follow Oddur's story.

'...but this was the only thing that I actually always found it hard to forgive him for...'

He asked Oddur what he was talking about.

'You were so little you probably don't even remember it. But I stole some money once from the register at the shop. The old man caught me right away, knew exactly how much I had taken. I was so ashamed I swore I would never steal again, even stopped snatching rhubarb from Jóna's garden. Old man didn't take it too badly, but what do you know? Before you know it he accuses me of stealing again. But this time I was completely innocent. But he was just as convinced as the first time, even claimed to know how much. I hadn't touched the money, didn't even occur to me. But this time he really let me have it; he raged and ranted at me for an eternity. Docked my allowance for months and never seemed to want to let the thing go. And I was innocent, for Christ's sake!

'I've sometimes wondered whether that incident didn't shape my destiny, whether that's when my wheel of ill fortune began turning. Because after that I felt like it didn't matter how I behaved or performed, I would always be prejudged. I would always be thought dishonest.'

'You're not dishonest, Oddur, I've never thought so. You just like the sauce and don't know how to handle money.' Ólafur could feel the quiver in his voice.

Suddenly two men and a woman joined them; barrelling drunkenly into the pub and greeting Oddur with great enthusiasm. Ólafur was going to say goodnight, but Oddur got him to sit down and join the group that now merged in the corner. Ólafur called home and spoke to Steinunn, who had no objection to his staying out late; she was always in favour of his strengthening ties with family and friends.

Around midnight, Ólafur was on his fourth beer. He hadn't drunk this much since his fortieth birthday party last year. He chatted with the blonde girl, who seemed thrilled to hear that he ran a company. She said she wanted to study business administration, since she was fed up with being broke. But she had only half finished her secondary school diploma, even though she was 22 years old. 'You never have enough money to go to school, but if you don't go to school you can't make any money,' she said.

When Ólafur took a cab home around two in the morning he had the girl's phone number. He didn't plan on calling her, though. The number was just a part of the night's amusements.

II

Ólafur wasn't hung-over the following day, but he still felt miserable. The father's old castigations and Oddur's tearful protests echoed in his mind. He saw his child's hands bury a Mackintosh tin in the beach sand. For several weeks, he had no rest from such thoughts, which mingled with guilt over his infidelities. He felt suffocated by others' belief that he was good and by having to live alone with the secrets of old sins.

What was strange was that the only thing that could push these thoughts from his mind was the thought of the blonde girl at the pub. One day he punched her number into his mobile several times but each time decided against calling. The following day, he rang her up, but she didn't answer. He was relieved. An hour later she returned his call and said she had seen the number on her phone. He told her who he was, and said that he had so enjoyed their conversation that evening that he had wanted to talk to her a bit more. She neither seemed surprised nor did her voice betray that she had expected his call. He suggested lunch the next day. She asked where she should meet him, but he said he would prefer to pick her up.

He invited her to the lunch buffet at a hotel restaurant. She didn't take anything but a little bit of salad and a Diet Coke. She lit up a menthol cigarette before she had finished eating. He wasn't hungry himself, too excited over what he hoped he had in store, but he ate nonetheless to make sure that he didn't betray anything. He tried to pick up where they had left off before in the Kópavogur pub, asked whether she had started thinking about future studies, told her about a contract he was trying to finalise. But the conversation was stiff now, as if the girl had lost all interest in these matters, and he suspected that he had proceeded too fast, that she was getting cold feet. Still, she didn't seem nervous, just rather distant and restrained.

Nevertheless Ólafur had a hunch that his instincts hadn't failed him, although he didn't rule out the possibility that he was kidding himself. He took the chance during an unusually long silence just after he had finished eating, and said simply, 'I have a room here. Would you like to come up with me?' This suddenly brought the girl to life: 'Wow, I bet the rooms in this place are really nice!' she said and looked around at the paintings in the dining room and up at the chandeliers.

'Yeah, they're all right,' he said, a little surprised. She said she had once stayed in a five-star hotel with her aunt in London, which had been amazing. He in turn told her about a few hotels he had stayed in abroad, good and bad. Before he knew it they were having the liveliest chat about hotels, and now there was nothing embarrassing in the least about walking up to scope out the room in direct continuation of the conversation.

'Gosh, this is big and cosy,' said the girl when they stepped inside. Then he suddenly felt there had been enough chatting, and embraced her. She jumped and hesitated, but a moment later she responded to his kiss. Her caresses were submissive but devoid of passion. He thought about how magnificent it would be to have a young, naked, and strange female body in his hands, but somehow he couldn't fully realise this feeling, any more than he usually could. As though ecstasy were a mirage.

When he was getting dressed, a pack of condoms fell

out of his jacket pocket. They had been forgotten in the heat of the action. He sometimes had the horrible thought that he might become infected with an STD and pass it to Steinunn. Now he had to trust that nothing of the sort had happened and think about something else. The thought made him feel that he was losing control.

III

An uneventful interval followed, and Ólafur's guilty conscience slowly faded. For a long while he didn't feel the least desire for other women, and he gradually came to believe that he wouldn't cheat again. He thought to himself that he must have been meant to quit before it was too late, because life and the world had decided that he was good, and public opinion gradually becomes truth, since the truth that is bound up in silent secrets is worth little, doesn't really exist.

About a year after the evening at the Kópavogur pub, the letter arrived. It was pure coincidence that he should find it before Steinunn did, as she usually came home from work before he did and sorted the mail before he arrived. He found it at lunchtime, as it happened. He was used to spending his lunch hour at restaurants, in meetings, or at the office cafeteria. But today he had needed to go home to fetch some documents he had forgotten to bring along that morning.

Letters and flyers lay at his feet by the front door. He tossed the booklets in the bin and was going to leave the letters unopened on the kitchen bench when he spied the name of a law office on one of the envelopes. His name was typewritten on the front of it. He tore the letter open:

Mr. Ólafur Oddsson

I have been approached by a Ms. Sigrún Eva
Óskarsdóttir, National Registry No. 191181-2899,
who names you as the father of a girl child born to her
last February 15th. On her behalf, a demand is made
that you pay monthly child support from the child's
birth until its eighteenth birthday.

It is clear that a blood test will be required to
determine the child's paternity. A copy of this letter has
been sent to the Reykjavík District Commissioner.
Sincerely,
Svava Þórðardóttir, District Court Attorney

At first it was as illusory as a dream. Then he was consumed
with a silent terror. But desperation didn't overpower him.
His mind immediately began hunting for a solution. Of
course none readily occurred to him.

He wanted to avoid getting a letter from the District
Commissioner as well, so he called in two days later and
requested an appointment.

The representative, a woman of about forty, greeted
him with a mocking expression that he didn't know whether
was real or imagined. He asked for coffee, as he had just got
up and hadn't had a morning cup yet, but she laughed sharply
and said: 'Coffee! There's nothing like that here.' And he,
a man who had been invited to countless friendly meetings
where he'd been offered myriad drinks, hot and cold, cakes,
confections, and snacks, sensed that here he was no guest, let
alone a guest of honour, but rather a sort of criminal.

He filled out a form and signed his consent for a blood
test. She told him, furthermore, to contact the Pathology
Research Institute and make an appointment there. When
the test results were in hand, the Commissioner would be
in touch. He asked to be called on his mobile or directly at
work, but not at home. The representative smirked.

He decided to investigate the circumstances at the

Research Institute before making an appointment. His purpose was unclear, but he wanted to postpone the test for a while and weigh his options, because after it there would be no turning back. He had begun wondering how he could keep the paternity secret from Steinunn, and toyed with the weak hope of finding a solution and escaping everything.

The place surprised him. He had instinctively expected whitewashed walls, counters and floors polished to a shine, a sterilised atmosphere, superiority and coldness. He automatically had a fearful reverence for a place where the truth about him could be revealed with scientific irrefutability. But the furniture in the lobby was worn and the walls were clad with old-fashioned wood panelling. Behind the information desk sat two older ladies sipping coffee. The handle was broken off one of the cups. One of the women rose and smiled at him. Her hair was completely grey, her expression friendly. A spring sun shone in through the window, as familiar as all the carefree hours that now seemed a thing of the past.

He asked the woman a question he already knew the answer to – whether this was where blood tests in paternity investigations were performed. He tried to sound simply curious, but the woman gave him no chance at that, seemed to assume that he was the one involved. On the other hand, she was so friendly and pleasant that it didn't bother him.

'You call, dear, and make an appointment. Give us your name and we find you on the list.'

'And then what?'

'You come at the appointed time and let the nurse take a blood sample. The results will be there in four or five weeks, and they go to the District Commissioner, who will be in touch with you.'

'And there's nothing else?'

'No dear, nothing else. It's quite simple, and best to get it out of the way as soon as possible.'

He felt lighter, but didn't know why. Something was

fermenting inside him; he sensed a solution but couldn't quite grasp it. Maybe he was just kidding himself. There still didn't seem to be any escape, but he no longer felt anxious.

IV

That evening Oddur called him. He hadn't done that in a long time. He sighed heavily over the phone, skipped all small talk, and cut straight to the chase: 'You probably know it's not easy for me to ask for your help, but I'm going to try now because I have nowhere else to go.'

Ólafur suggested a café for lunch the following day. Oddur named the place. Ólafur didn't ask for further details, but he was fairly certain of the substance of the request. Suddenly the solution came to him, and he realised it had been condensing from the time when he spoke to the old lady at the blood lab. He opened the wallet and took out all forms of identification. The pictures on the credit cards were too recent, but his driver's license and identity card were another matter. They might very well work.

He was surprised at the coincidence that Oddur should have to ask him for a loan at exactly this time. If it was a coincidence. The serious tone of Oddur's voice and words had indicated that he wasn't asking for small change this time. The general rule was that if Oddur asked for a big loan or needed him to co-sign a bill of exchange, Ólafur would give him five thousand krónur. If he asked for ten thousand, Ólafur would pay for his drinks and let that suffice. Oddur seemed to have given up ages ago on getting substantial sums out of his brother, who always drew the line firmly in such matters. This time he must either have used his sixth sense or be in more desperate straits than ever before.

V

They met at a sad café where a few grave-looking guests sat solitary and spread out across the room, too lost in their own thoughts to pay attention to the conversations of others. The air was heavy – not exactly smelly, but laced with something vaguely resembling a stench. They sat by the window, and a bus was reflected in the pane but never appeared on the street outside. For a brief while, Ólafur felt that existence was a lifeless shadow.

Oddur had no patience for preamble. As soon as Ólafur had fetched himself a cup of coffee and sat down, he came to the point. 'Listen, mate, I don't really expect you to agree to this, but right now my life depends on getting a bit of a loan somewhere, immediately if not sooner. And what's more, I can easily pay you back.'

'How much do you need?'

'If I don't have two hundred thousand tomorrow morning, I'm in really bad shape, straight-up terrible trouble, actually. But I'll get money at the end of the month, social security benefits and so on, in just a couple of weeks. So if I'm realistic and honest, I could pay the lot back in three months, three paydays, you see, benefit payments: pay you, live frugally on the rest.'

'You don't have to pay me anything. It so happens that I have a job for you to do, a job that you're just right for. It's an easy task, but an important one, and you're actually the only viable candidate for it.'

Suddenly Ólafur was ice cold and calm. It was a good feeling. When you have a well-developed plan, the plan takes over and pushes all unpleasant feelings aside.

Oddur tried to hide his surprise with an empty smile, but his face was one big question mark. Ólafur told him to pull out his ID. He studied the pictures on them for a long time before he told Oddur what he had in mind.

He tried to keep the story of his troubles as simple

and short as he could. Avoided meeting Oddur's eye while he spoke but saw from the corner of his eye how his facial expression changed, from attentiveness to surprise and from surprise to something resembling admiration. Then he explained his plan to Oddur.

'Well now. Never knew you had it in you,' Oddur said with wide eyes. 'I always thought you were the same old harmless angel. Even though I've always admired you in a certain way, dear bruv, you're sometimes a bit too perfect for my taste. To tell the truth, I didn't think you had the balls for something like this.'

'You call that balls? Knocking up some strange slip of a girl?'

'Men get into trouble, Ólafur. That's their nature. Men are beasts out of control. Women are the ones who prevent the world from going under. Some men control their wild nature by letting women control them, good women like your Steinunn, but beneath the surface their true nature is always hiding. You're living proof of it.'

Ólafur said he didn't have time to debate the nature of the sexes, but asked emphatically: 'Do we have a deal, then?'

Oddur nodded slowly and deeply. 'Oh yes. Oh yes indeed. I just can't believe you're going to pay me two hundred thousand krónur for taking your ID and donating a few drops of blood.'

'Trivial to you, important to me: that much is clear,' Ólafur said with impatience in his voice.

'But I need money right away, and this can hardly happen today?'

'I'll pay you three hundred thousand. You'll get two hundred thousand later today, and one hundred thousand when the results are in.'

Oddur laughed, quietly at first but then forcefully, with a touch of savagery. A bearded man in a dirty coat looked up from his paper and gazed sadly at them. The laughter abated suddenly and Oddur winked at Ólafur, who now noticed that he looked much the worse for wear since the last time they had met. Frankly, he looked frightfully bad. Ólafur didn't even want to contemplate what sort of people his brother's current creditors might be. Once upon a time Oddur had been a healthy boy who built backyard huts and gave Ólafur his old Matchbox cars when he bought new ones. Once they had both been normal, innocent boys. Now here they were, doing dark deeds in this twilight tableau.

Oddur's lips turned up in a grin. He took their identity cards off the table and held one in each hand so they faced Ólafur. 'To think, I've always felt that we were like black and white, but just look, we're actually damn similar.'

VI

In the ensuing days and weeks, a heavy weight was lifted off Ólafur's shoulders. He enjoyed good times with Steinunn and showed her more interest than he had for a long time. He thought to himself that you never knew what you had until you'd been at risk of losing it. Once they went swimming together, and while they swam side by side in adjacent lanes, the rain began pouring down. Steinunn shrieked and laughed like a little girl by the pool's edge, and suddenly Ólafur was struck that this must have happened before, maybe twenty years ago. He dove under the lane rope and resurfaced in Steinunn's arms. He embraced her and felt that the old memory that hung in the air didn't course through him, but just some sensation that resembled it: the lust was missing. Steinunn was security, familiarity, and warmth, but the lust would not return. How could that be expected, anyway? Ólafur thought to himself that people nowadays demanded everything. Wanted to have their cake and eat it too. Wanted warmth and security but also lust and excitement. And he had been no better than anyone else.

When the letter from the District Commissioner arrived, lucky chance would have it that he was the one to check the mail and not Steinunn. He had expected a phone call rather than a letter and hadn't watched the mail for it. It was just before noon on a Saturday, and he wasn't used to getting mail on Saturdays, though it happened every once in a while. Steinunn was at the gym, but he was still lying on his stomach in bed with the papers and his coffee when he heard the clanging of the letterbox. Their children, two teenagers, were at sports practice.

The contents of the letter took a long time to filter into his mind, which rejected the context of the words on the page. He hadn't digested the news when he took the letter into the bedroom, sat down on the bed, and read it again.

He read it several times more and muttered repeatedly, 'This is impossible; this is impossible.' There was discussion of the arrangements for child support payments and how to apply for visitation rights.

'Visitation rights?' he muttered in numb inquiry.

He wondered how this mistake could be possible and what he should do to correct it. Finally he realised what must have happened, and then he laughed. It was a loud, joyless laugh that died away abruptly.

He pondered the meaning of the results. Since this matter had come up, he had by turns told himself that he was meant to reveal his secrets or to live with them. Without thinking about it, he had assumed that there was a purpose to existence. Now he suddenly realised that there was no purpose. The only answer the question about purpose evoked was a mental image of the confused fellow with the grey belly, at the bar in Kópavogur, the evening he met Oddur and saw the blonde girl for the first time. Suddenly he felt that his entire being was reflected in this man: clueless and pointless amid so many blind coincidences. And he saw in his mind's eye this blind stupidity carved into Oddur's unsuspecting face, he who had no idea that he had disproved that he was the father of his own child. Doubtless he was sunk deep into his own worries, as usual, thinking them the only ones in the world.

The Birthday Present

In late April of 1973, a forty-year-old doctor, Guðjón Guðbjartsson by name, received a strange phone call. An index finger had travelled down the middle column of page 197 of the phone directory, past one Guðjón after the other, until it stopped by the identically named Guðjón Guðbjartsson, physician, and Guðjón Guðbjartsson, master metalworker.

Though the incident was hardly worth noting, even completely unremarkable, it stayed with the doctor, and it took him several weeks to put it from his mind. On the phone was a voice that seemed to belong to a teenage girl. The voice was hesitant, perhaps even fearful, and the breathing heavy: 'Is this Guðjón Guðbjartsson?' – 'Yes, this is he,' replied the doctor. A long silence followed, and he heard the child swallow saliva. At the moment when one usually says 'Who is this?' in such a conversation, followed by 'Hello, hello ... who is this, hello,' Guðjón let slip the following curious question: 'Is that you, Dagn"?' – he heard quiet whispering on the line, as if the children were now two or more together, and a moment later the line went dead.

The whispering towards the end was reassuring, since it indicated that this was just some sort of prank. That was the only explanation. On the other hand, he hadn't sensed any of the mirth that accompanies such teasing; the voice and the silence had rather seemed tense and charged. But the child's voice was startlingly similar to that of one of Guðjón's patients, a girl who had died of leukaemia shortly before. Her name was Dagn", and she was the daughter of a close friend of Guðjón's. He had been the girl's doctor for two years, and her death had hit him harder than that of any other patient; he was at once the child's physician and mourner.

That same evening, the metalworker Guðjón Guðbjartsson received a considerably more important phone call. Guðjón, who was 38 years old, was informed that he had become the father of a little girl. He had sat at home all evening, nervous and excited, but now he drove as fast as he could up to the maternity ward. There he got to see and hold his fourth child. As well as the newborn girl, he had two young boys with his wife. But in addition, Guðjón had a nineteen-year-old daughter whom he had never beheld and didn't even know existed. Even less did he suspect that his eldest child had the same birthday as his newborn girl. The daughter he didn't know existed was born on April 23, 1954.

I

The spring of 1972 was a time of great growth for Jóhanna's family. Jóhanna was going on 11 years old at the time. Her father worked a day job in the warehouse of a large wholesale distributor, and at night he did various types of extra work that she knew little about. Actually, he had always been so hard-working that she hardly knew him and was both shy and a bit scared of him, as though he were merely a houseguest with no interest in children. But now there were tangible signs in the air that his industriousness was beginning to pay off.

The mother, who had worked half-days in a cafeteria for as long as Jóhanna could remember, started working there full time and took on cleaning the place a few nights a week. Eiríkur, Jóhanna's elder brother, quit during his first year at the Technical College that winter and began working for the Steel Furniture Company. Every week he brought home the latest pop songs on 45 rpm records that he let Jóhanna share with him, and she played them on the Blaupunkt stereo in the living room, sometimes dancing to them with friends, sometimes singing along in home-grown English. That summer Eiríkur bought a fancy new stereo for his own room. It came with a large, plush pair of headphones that he allowed Jóhanna to use, so she could listen to the records on the new stereo whenever she wanted when he wasn't home. He also began inviting her regularly for rides downtown, buying her a hot dog and a Coke. Once he sent her with 500 krónur into a toy shop, where she enjoyed a magical time and emerged with a shop register and a merchant who sat at the register with a chair attached to it, wearing a white cap with a visor and smiling broadly.

Time after time that spring, large and small delivery cars followed Dad home in the evening, and from them emerged various things that gradually made the household grand, especially the living room. First came a brown sofa with plush upholstery: a sturdy sofa in place of the old teak one with the worn wool covering, and two chairs opposite it. Between the chairs and the sofa came a new coffee table, beautifully carved and with lathe-turned legs. Next was a light brown rocking chair, intended for the head of the family, though Dad rarely sat in it. The Hansa shelves were screwed off the walls and in their place came an enormous shelf-and-cabinet unit with glass doors and a TV cabinet. One evening, a large palisander bookcase was brought in and the shelves lined with the complete works of Halldór Laxness. Dad also bought a lovely newspaper rack made of pale wood and a transistor radio for the kitchen window.

New carpets were laid; thick wool carpets for the living and dining rooms. And because they were harder to vacuum, a new and more advanced Nilfisk vacuum cleaner was bought.

Still, none of this was as exciting to Jóhanna as her parents' new bed: it had two built-in ashtrays and a radio with a clock that told the time with green numbers and a colon on a dark screen. In the evenings, Mum often smoked in bed and listened to the radio; on rare occasions Dad would join her and they sometimes lay fully dressed on top of the bedspread with cups of coffee on the little nightstands that were attached to the bed, a story or a play on the radio and sometimes pop songs on the station from the American base at Keflavík, mixed with crackling static.

Sometimes Jóhanna fetched the transistor radio from the kitchen, switched it on in her bedroom and pretended that it was attached to the bed.

The evenings were often lonely, but if she furtively stayed up late enough, she could enjoy observing the coffee conversations in the kitchen. Usually it was just Mum and Eiríkur, chatting about work over coffee and a cigarette, sometimes Dad as well, and on rare occasions there were guests. Watching the kitchen conversations was not unlike watching television, as the grownups rarely paid her any attention.

II

The first car that Eiríkur bought was a pale green 1957 Chevrolet Bel Air. The car was hardly driven at all after the first week, and it mostly stood untouched in the old garage on the back lot, which had once been a barn. Eiríkur never managed to make it really roadworthy, though the unmuffled droning of the engine could occasionally be heard in the neighbourhood. Nevertheless, Eiríkur steadfastly maintained that he had never owned a better car. He often cursed his other cars, even though they were all drivable. The Volkswagen Beetle was far too small, 'a total sardine can'. Eiríkur bought and sold a brown Cortina and an off-white Taunus in short order. Both cars were fairly new and didn't give any trouble, but Eiríkur couldn't stand either of them, called them European hunks of junk. Finally he bought a red Saab that he neither praised nor censured but settled with silently.

All along, the Chevrolet stood in the garage, and for a long time Eiríkur attended to it whenever he had the chance.

Once Jóhanna saw him pat the hood of the car affectionately. This was the best car. Jóhanna agreed with Eiríkur, but she hadn't a clue why. She imagined a family that always spent evenings and weekends together, took long car rides in this beautiful pale green car and sometimes camped out in the countryside. The car gleamed in the sunlit summer night, and when the family had fallen asleep in the tent a little bird perched on the hood. Together the car and the bird watched over the sleeping people all night.

III

Jóhanna never heard her parents argue, but then she didn't see them together very often. One weekend late in August she heard her mother say, 'Then go, damn you.' A moment later the father emerged expressionless from the kitchen, took a seat in the living room, and picked a newspaper up from the wooden rack. In the kitchen, the mother stirred away at the contents of a pot as if nothing had happened. Jóhanna thought to herself that she must have misheard.

A few days later, yet another delivery truck appeared outside their house, the first one in several months, as a matter of fact. Jóhanna wondered how more furniture could possibly fit inside and waited in anticipation to see what might emerge from the vehicle. But instead the van was loaded with the brown sofa, the shelf unit, the rocking chair, the fancy bed, the radio from the kitchen, and two stuffed suitcases. In the living room, the old, worn teak sofa with the wool covering reappeared. Where on Earth had it been kept? It was strange to see it here again, like going back in time by an entire year.

A while later, Mum woke her in the middle of the night and said: 'Can't you sleep, Jóhanna dear?' Jóhanna had been fast asleep, but this woke her up completely. Mum walked her into the master bedroom and they went to sleep on a large mattress that lay on the floor in place of a bed. Jóhanna looked up at the ceiling and sensed an old memory that didn't take form in her mind. Sometime, long ago, she had lain between the two of them in that bed.

IV

In the fall, girls started appearing in Eiríkur's red Saab. The first two girls he seemed to meet in rapid succession, and they vanished just as quickly. They never came in with him, but waited in the car while he popped in to change clothes for a dance or a party, fetch something that he had forgotten, or even wolf down cold food in a great hurry.

The former had short, light red hair, a chubby face and freckles, but the latter had long, dark, wavy hair and high cheekbones. But even though the girls were quite different in appearance, their mannerisms were so similar that they almost became a single person in Jóhanna's mind, or more precisely a certain guise that she began to believe was shared by all young women who drove out with young men: silent, polite and slightly grumpy-looking under a heavy layer of makeup; didn't move in their seats but sometimes shot shy glances this way and that.

The next time Eiríkur asked her out for a ride, she snuck into her mother's makeup, rouged her cheeks, coloured her lips, and darkened her eyelids. She wasn't used to applying makeup, and her reflection looked more like a clown than a fine lady, but she didn't let that stop her. She sat stiff and silent in the front seat the entire ride, and when Eiríkur invited her into a shop she declined politely, even though she desperately wanted a Coke and a hot dog or some sweets. Instead she sat hunched over in the car while he was in the shop and glanced shyly at passers-by. She enjoyed the game for a moment, but then the loneliness overwhelmed her. When Eiríkur returned to the car she asked him bluntly:

'Where is Dad, anyway?' For one moment she felt as if she had entered forbidden territory, without knowing why, and her heart skipped a beat. But Eiríkur answered without hesitation:

'In Akureyri.'

'Is that where the Skagi football team plays?' she asked, though she had no interest in football.

'No,' said Eiríkur. 'That's Akranes. Akureyri is a larger town, way up north, where everything is drowning in snow and people ski cross-country to get everywhere. And there are big forests up there, bigger than up in Heiðmörk.'

Sometimes she imagined that she and Eiríkur were a married couple. That she worked in a toy shop and came home from work before him and cooked his dinner. Once she actually tried to cook for him. Mum had popped home for dinner, warmed up some instant soup, made sandwiches, and gone back out to her cleaning job. When she had left, Jóhanna cooked three eggs and some liver sausage on a skillet. The eggs were supposed to be fried, but the yolks ran together and burned slightly, forming some sort of omelette; the liver sausage also smelled rather strange. Then everything went cold on the skillet. Though it didn't look very good, she was so wrapped up in her game that she was convinced Eiríkur would eat it all up with pleasure, or at least she was until she heard the sound of the front door. Then she jumped and suddenly wished she could destroy the evidence.

She stood in front of the skillet while Eiríkur sat at the kitchen table, smoked, and sighed with fatigue. A while later Mum came home and asked Eiríkur whether she should heat the soup for him. But he wasn't hungry, had eaten at Múli Café on his way home. Jóhanna stood in front of the stove until Mum told her to get to bed. Then she ran into her room and waited for the consequences, convinced that she would be scolded.

When she came home from school shortly after noon the next day, everything still lay untouched on the skillet.

It was as if Eiríkur and Mum hadn't even noticed. All she had to do was scrape the contents into the bin to completely escape punishment.

She wasn't relieved, but instead felt strangely empty inside.

V

For a short while, Eiríkur's red Saab was womanless, and Jóhanna eagerly awaited the arrival of a new girl. In November, two girls appeared, Lísa and Björg. They wore no makeup and weren't shy at all, and they never hid out in the car but came in for coffee with Eiríkur. Evening after evening, they sat in the kitchen with him and sometimes Mum as well, drank coffee, smoked, and chatted. Lísa was tall and strong-looking while Björg was small and chubby. Lísa was loud, but Björg spoke quietly. Still, there was something about Björg that made people pay more attention to her and listen to her, perhaps because her tone of voice demanded careful listening. When Jóhanna listened to the kitchen conversation from the living room or her bedroom, she could always hear Lísa the best, but whenever the group fell silent she knew that Björg was talking. As it happened, it was when Björg arrived on the scene that Jóhanna began avoiding the kitchen when the coffee conversation was going on: she could no longer expect to be ignored. She had grown used to the adults' paying her no attention, but Björg was different: she was always looking at her, offering her a seat at the table, and asking her questions, some of them embarrassing, like whether she had a boyfriend or liked a boy. It reminded her of a fizzy tablet that she had once put in her mouth instead of dissolving it in water. The flavour was much too strong, so she couldn't enjoy it, even though she liked it when the powder from the pill was mixed with water. When Björg looked at her and spoke to her, Jóhanna looked away and wanted to run and hide. Nevertheless, there were few things she liked more than this attention; she enjoyed it afterwards and waited with excitement for Björg to return.

Gradually, her shyness faded, and Jóhanna became more forward in the kitchen. Björg had her sit beside her and gave her milk mixed with some coffee. Jóhanna began to talk so much that Eiríkur thought enough was enough. When Mum wasn't at home, she sometimes got to have a smoke, and once she smoked an entire cigarette, after which she spent an hour on the sofa in cold sweats and never touched tobacco again.

Once they all watched a Chaplin film together on TV. In the middle of a fit of laughter, Lísa slung her head backward and bumped it sharply on the windowsill behind her. She howled with pain, but burst out laughing again a moment later, took another backward dive, and hit the windowsill again. Then all the others laughed, and Lísa was suddenly funnier than Chaplin on the screen.

Lísa didn't come back after this, and as time went by, Jóhanna began to imagine that the laughing over the encounter with the windowsill had turned to crying, even to piercing headaches and insomnia during the night. From time to time she even imagined that Lísa hadn't survived the incident, and though she knew it was rubbish, she didn't dare ask about her.

Björg, on the other hand, became an increasingly more frequent guest. Once Jóhanna walked in on her and Eiríkur in a deep kiss on the sofa. She stiffened up, her throat went dry, and black spots danced before her eyes. Of course this had to happen. She had known it, but she hadn't known that she knew it.

She liked Björg too well to build up any antipathy towards her over this development. She accepted seeing her barefoot in a terry bathrobe in the kitchen in the mornings, and ate the bread she toasted for her. She accepted having to wait for her to finish in the bathroom. She even tolerated the snogging, which seemed to be on the increase.

But the day when Eiríkur's stereo, bed, desk, chair, old model airplanes and various other stuff were all carried out into yet another moving truck, which was parked outside the house, she had had enough. She glared hatefully at Eiríkur and screamed: 'You're going to Akureyri, you bastard!'

She charged out of the house, ran blindly away at first, but then headed towards the deserted hill on the edge of the neighbourhood. But when she sensed that she wasn't about to cry and so didn't need to hide behind a big rock, she turned around and walked slowly back with a glare on her face, biting her lips together. A cold wind was in from the north, but the icy breeze didn't affect her, even though she was only wearing a sweater. She was too angry to feel cold; she probably wouldn't even have felt pain if a rock had struck her head. It was a Saturday, nearly three o'clock. It was still light out, and the faint winter sun misted the clouds; at noon it had flooded in through the windows. The Christmas snow had been slowly melting in the past weeks, but the frost preserved ice and some hard snow here and there.

She snuck into the yard behind her house, and hoped that somebody was in the windows to see how angry she looked. Their house had been a farm once; the barns and stables had mostly been torn down, except for the one that still stood as a garage and the old cowshed that stood mostly empty as before. They had used it to store old stuff, and the teak sofa had probably been kept there last year without her noticing. Now her parents' old bed, from before dad moved the modern one in and out, caught her eye. She hadn't seen that bed in almost a year, but it seemed to hail from another life or a lost time, like the stories of farmers, cows, and sheep here in the area. Once she had caught a faint cow smell in here, but now it was gone; the cowshed was odourless, just full of cold air.

When she was born, the neighbourhood was growing

rapidly; houses were multiplying and streets were being paved. Their house was probably the oldest one in the vicinity. She wasn't thinking about this per se, since she didn't really have the facts straight, but when she looked around herself now, she had a wordless feeling of how everything wore away and changed. Her father had called her from time to time a few months after he moved away. They were awkward phone calls; he pretended to be interested in a variety of things that he had never asked her about before: school, friends, the pop records she listened to in the living room. She hadn't regretted his moving away, but after the phone call she felt an awakening nostalgia, an unclear memory of half-forgotten times: a close-knit family and parents who spoke kindly to her when she was little.

Suddenly she wanted to look at the pale green Chevrolet. She hadn't done that for a long time. She walked to the open garage, but the Chevrolet had vanished. The garage was completely empty.

VI

The kitchen in the basement flat on Kjartansgata was much smaller than the kitchen at home. It wasn't even a kitchen, really, just a corner. People could hardly sit down, drink coffee, smoke, and chat; there was no way an onlooker could have enough space to stay just off to the side and listen to the conversation.

But rarely had anyone been so happy with such an unimposing space as Björg was in this case. And Jóhanna was determined to have just such a tiny little kitchen when she herself started keeping house. Björg opened a little wall cabinet with a side door and proudly showed Jóhanna her plates and glasses, pulled out pots and a pan from a cabinet under the bench, turned on a ring on the little stove and put the kettle on, hummed a tune and put slices of bread in the toaster.

'This is my dream,' she said with a faraway smile. 'I've always wanted to keep house in my own place.'

'Are you going to have kids?' Jóhanna asked.

'Of course. Then you'll be big auntie.'

'But aren't you worried that he'll leave you later when the kids are grown up?'

Björg looked at her for a long time and said: 'No, he won't. I'm going to take such good care of him that he always wants to stay with me.'

It was strange for Jóhanna to hear her speak this way about her brother, but it didn't make her jealous. At first Jóhanna had been furious at Björg and sworn a silent oath never to speak to her again, but Björg had either ignored her anger or not noticed it. It was tiring to be angry for a long time if nobody paid any attention to you. Her expression of righteous indignation was impressive enough in the bathroom mirror, but it didn't seem to bother anyone. And Björg was always so interested in her, for whatever reason, that avoiding her wasn't the most appealing prospect.

Granted, Eiríkur had always been kind to her, but his kindness was an absent-minded and distant generosity. Mum was neither good nor bad. Nobody was mean. But at some point all of them had started living in their own worlds, be it at home, in Akureyri, or on Kjartansgata. Now Mum was visited in the evenings by a rather old man who wore a suit and sported a moustache, preferred drinking coffee in the living room rather than the kitchen, and smoked cigars and not cigarettes. The cigars smelled good, but Mum didn't want Jóhanna in the living room when the man was visiting, so she had scant opportunity to observe him and he paid her no attention.

'We'll celebrate my birthday here in April,' said Björg. 'You and your mum will be invited, of course. Just think! A birthday party in my own apartment! I can't wait!'

But Jóhanna wasn't thinking about a birthday party. She nodded with a smile, staring all the while at the little kitchen table in the corner. There she saw Eiríkur and Björg in her mind's eye, having dinner in the future with two children, a boy and a girl. Eiríkur and Björg's faces were blurry, but she gave Eiríkur her mum's friend's moustache to make him look older. The children's faces were clear, though: they were Eiríkur and herself.

VII

On a Wednesday night, a few days before the birthday party, Björg came alone for a visit. It was late April, winter was over, and it stayed light into the evenings. Jóhanna felt like it was years since last spring, because everything had changed this winter. When Björg rang the doorbell the dusk was pale blue on the windows.

Mum wasn't at home; she was at the cinema with the cigar man. Afterwards they might have a drink at a big bar like in the films on TV. Jóhanna asked about Eiríkur. Björg said she wanted to be alone with her. Jóhanna half-filled a glass of milk, added coffee and lots of sugar. Björg sipped her coffee black, an incomprehensible taste that Jóhanna was nevertheless determined to acquire later.

Björg bore an expression that was secretive and demanding at the same time. 'Do you know what I want most of all for my birthday?' she asked.

'I can give you a birthday present,' Jóhanna said eagerly. 'I have three hundred krónur in notes in a little cardboard box and lots of change.'

'But guess what I want.'

'Mmm... you want something new for your kitchen.' Björg smiled and shook her head. Then she corrected her gesture:

'Yeah, sure, but not the most.'

'You want new jeans and a pretty statue for the living room window.'

'No, not the most.'

Björg stood up and bent over to pick up a plastic bag she had left on the kitchen floor. She didn't seem very fat from the front, but her behind became quite large when she bent over, groaning. She took a layer cake and half a length of Vienna bread from the bag, laid them on the kitchen counter along with a cutting board, and cut the treats into little slices. Then she placed the cutting board with all the goodies on the kitchen table.

'I thought the two of us could have a little birthday party now.'

'But the birthday's on Saturday.'

'No, the party's then, but my birthday is today. It's April 23rd. I was born on this day in 1954.'

Jóhanna was good at mental arithmetic and said: 'Are you 19? Then you're older than Eiríkur.'

'Yes. Half a year older. Do you think that's strange?'

'No. Or I don't know. I just thought somehow that he was older because he's the man but you're the woman. What is it that you want for a birthday present?'

'What I want most for a birthday present doesn't cost any money.'

'No money? What is it, then?'

'I want to hear my dad's voice.'

'Your dad's voice? Where is your dad?' Jóhanna had only ever seen Björg's mother, but for some reason she hadn't thought at all about who or where her father might be.

'I've never seen him.'

'Never seen him?'

'I know what his name is. The name is in the phone book. The only thing my mum has ever been willing to tell me is his name.'

'And do you think he'll call you on your birthday?'

'No. He can't. He doesn't know I exist. Mum didn't tell him because they didn't know each other very well and she didn't know where he was. I think he was abroad studying medicine when I was born.'

'Is your dad a doctor?'

'Jóhanna.' Björg fixed her with a firm and supplicating stare. 'You can give me this birthday gift. I've always wanted to call him, but I don't dare. I don't know why. I'm not planning to talk to him, I just want to hear the voice. And even though it's silly, I don't dare do it unless someone else calls and asks whether it's him or asks him to come to the phone. His name is Guðjón Guðbjartsson. He's in the phone book. I haven't even dared look at the number because I don't want to memorise it and accidentally call him because I'd thought about the number too much and couldn't control myself.'

'But what should I say to him?'

'Just ask whether he's available. Say his name. And let me listen and hear the voice.'

After the phone call, Jóhanna asked whether Björg was sure her father was a doctor. Whether he couldn't just as well be a metalworker, and therefore be the other Guðjón Guðbjartsson. Björg said she really didn't know, but that she had always thought of him as a doctor. Jóhanna suggested that they call the metalworker as well because then Björg would definitely have heard her father's voice.

'I feel like I've already heard it,' Björg said. She was suddenly shy, and it was impossible to tell whether the phone call had made her happy or sad.

'In that case, you probably have a sister named Dagn",' said Jóhanna. 'He thought I was Dagn".' She dialled the metalworker's number, but nobody picked up.

Then she turned to the Akureyri section and found her father's name and phone number after some search. He hadn't called since Christmas. She'd received an over-sized sweater from him as a Christmas present. Two packages had come from up north, one for her and another for Eiríkur. Eiríkur got a sweater as well, one that was only slightly larger than hers; it was too small for him.

Jóhanna let her finger rest on her father's name in the directory and tried to imagine his environment. She saw a wooden house in a forest where the trees were covered with snow.

She closed the phone book and asked Björg about more birthday presents. They talked for a long time as the windows went dark.

Lunch Break, 1976

I COME HOME unusually hung-over; can't bear to stay at work any longer. Going to use this contractual hour off to rest in safety and solitude so I can suffer through the afternoon, finish the projects and tolerate glances, imagined or real. Still, it's often so miserable to step in through the door here at lunchtime, see the untouched rubbish that you had in front of your eyes in the morning: coats in the front hall, the kids' toys on the floor. But I've told myself that everything's going to be fine now, probably nobody home, I can throw myself on the sofa, close my eyes, and be alone in the world for just under an hour. I should head straight for the living room, but I step into the kitchen because my stomach hurts - didn't eat any breakfast - and I decide to wolf down some dry bread or crackers to fill it up a bit before my nap. I still dread what I may see in the kitchen and how it will affect my mood.

To my surprise the sink is empty. She must have done the dishes this morning. For some reason this doesn't please me; instead, I get annoyed, as if the sink were chock full of dishes encrusted with hardened scraps of food. The feeling is more along the lines of: *it's too good to be true, something must be behind this.* And then one gets even more annoyed than if the sink had been full. The pots are still standing on the stove but not in the cupboard where they belong, and I wonder whether she cleaned them as well or was planning to let the leftovers go bad in them in their own good time. The big pot turns out to be empty and squeaky clean. But the potato pot is half-full of water and in it is half a sheep's

73

head! Never have I seen anything but potatoes in this pot. This is ridiculous, and anger begins to boil inside me. Has the woman finally taken leave of her senses?

I'm planning to head for the telephone and let her have it. Looking forward to it. She's always humbler and fairer over than phone than she is face to face. She always plays a polished and contented person at work and probably doesn't want anyone to hear her raise her voice. I rush into the living room and have already snatched up the receiver by the time I remember that it's never possible to reach her during lunch. I grit my teeth and my knuckles whiten around the phone. For a brief moment the thought strikes me that this is a stratagem on her part. She knew I had a horrible hangover this morning, worse than usual, and she knows that I sometimes come home at lunch and take a nap when I'm feeling under the weather. Was there a better way to take revenge on me than this? Making me think that everything was just right, empty sink and so on, and then this disgustingly absurd spectacle that I was probably supposed to stumble upon just as peace of mind seemed within my grasp. And we both know I can't reach her at lunchtime. Cruelty perfected!

Suddenly I hear children's voices. They seem to emanate from the kitchen. The voices grow louder and clearer when I enter the room, but of course there is no one there. They are carried in through the open window. Two or three girls seem to be standing by the wall and chatting. Probably my daughter and her friends. Upon hearing them I realise that it won't have been my wife who put the head in the potato pot after all; it must have been the girl! On reflection, boiling a sheep's head in a potato pot is such a childish deed that it resonates far more with a child's mischief than a woman's stratagem.

I'm about to head out and give her a piece of my mind, but something persuades me to stay a moment and listen to the girls – a vague notion of preserving my solitude and thereby the hope of a bit of rest and peace. I listen for my daughter's voice, but either she's not participating in the conversation or I can't tell her voice from the others'. Maybe she isn't there, maybe these are just strangers.

'If soldiers came and were going to shoot us I would hide under my mattress.' - Isn't that her voice? What is she doing blathering on about soldiers? On top of everything else, I'll teach her not to be spouting rubbish by the house wall like this. - 'There are only good soldiers in Iceland; they're in Keflavík and they take care of us.' - Is *this* her, perhaps? I actually think both voices resemble hers, even though they don't particularly resemble each other.

I immediately cease to make out what the girls are saying, since I have no interest at all in their chit-chat. A sudden stillness comes over me. I can't help but feel that there's something enchanting about hearing the girls' conversation without their knowing I'm here and without my knowing whether my daughter is on the other side of the wall. Some vague notion of being able to witness my family's life and my own without taking part in it. I begin to imagine what will happen when I go outside. 'Were you cooking in the pot?' I will call. But she denies it flat out. That makes me even more furious. 'You're not just disobedient, but a liar as well,' I scream. I seize her by the collar and drag her into the house. She pretends to be terrified, screams bloody murder, and acts as if I'm abusing her. I'm forced to shake her vigorously and slap her to quiet her down and get her to listen to me. And the blows may continue until she stops screaming, hanging by her joints, and raises herself up, grows silent, looks at the potato pot and confesses to the deed. But what if she doesn't stop screaming? What if she keeps screaming as the blows increase in number? I can't back down, can I?

'Were you cooking in the pot?' I say a bit less loudly than I did the first time around. I fix her with a stern gaze but haven't quite erupted in fury, perhaps because her friends are here. - 'Yes, I had a little bite of sheep's head,' she says softly.

('A bite of sheep's head' is exactly the phrase she would use.)
In her eyes is a heartfelt plea: let this be all right, say it isn't
forbidden, say at the very least that it isn't a grave offence.
And despite my determination to the contrary, I can feel
my anger evaporate beneath her gaze. I hesitate, and there
is a brief moment of silence. 'Well, all right, but you can't
use the potato pot to boil sheep's heads. It's only for boiling
potatoes. Remember that next time.' – She nods. 'And you
have to remember to turn off the stove if you really must be
cooking these things for yourself.' – She cheers up at this,
becomes eager, and almost trips over her words: 'Yes, I did
remember, I took special care to turn off the stove.' – 'Yes,
it was good of you to remember that.' – I've started praising
her instead of scolding. What a mess. At least I can take some
consolation from her having told the truth and reaped as she
sowed in that regard.

I'm probably not in any condition to have a fight like
this now. It may have to await a better time.

The girls have fallen silent. I hadn't noticed. I perk my
ears but can't hear anything except the sound of a distant car.
They have probably left. Now it's as if they had not been
there and the conversation had never taken place. A strange,
dreamlike loneliness settles over me: I see myself years from
now, sitting at a table in a cafeteria, a white plastic cup and
a half-eaten doughnut on a piece of cardboard in front of
me. By the table rests a grey metal crutch, and I am tired
and listless. For a brief moment it is as if I am situated in this
future and the present incident is just a faded memory.

The time is ten minutes past twelve. With each minute,
my hope of a good midday nap grows weaker. But to tell the
truth, I don't feel quite so miserable anymore. In the blink
of an eye, my condition has changed from pure agony to a
normal, everyday hangover.

I fish the head up out of the potato pot. It's an unusually
dark one, which further corroborates my suspicion that this is
my daughter's handiwork; she didn't have the sense to scrape

it. I put it on a plate and in the refrigerator, rinse out the pot and dry it. I have cleaned a pot here in the kitchen before, but I can't recall when it was.

My stomach starts growling; it sounds like static on a radio. Not only is my stomach empty, I am actually downright hungry. I begin by looking for bread, but then I have a flash of inspiration, open the fridge, take out the plate with the sheep's head, and sit down at the table.

Why did the girl not eat anything, since she went to the trouble of boiling it? The head hasn't been touched. No wonder, perhaps, when a child is involved, but it hasn't escaped anyone's notice in this household that the girl loves sheep's heads. Especially sheep's tongue. 'Daddydaddy, can I have the tongue, mummymummy, can I have the tongue?' is the constant refrain when we have sheep's heads for dinner.

Sometimes a diabolical mood turns to glee at a moment's notice. Most often the change occurs when I have a drink; I'm always happiest on my first glass. But it happens that the joy comes upon me in the midst of my agony without my having had a drop. Then it's as if I'm drunk on something other than alcohol. It's rare, but I can feel it happening now. All of a sudden I have developed a tickling sensation in my stomach. There is something comical about the sheep's head and my daughter.

It isn't until I turn it over that I laugh so loud it echoes throughout the empty house. The head is missing its tongue.

After the Summer House

July 1998

EVERY SUMMER WE go to Erna's childhood village. Shortly before we drive into town we can see the unimposing settlement by the fjord; it looks like an old photograph of the place rather than the village itself as it stands now, as it appears up close. The image vanishes as we drive up the hill, the ocean and the shore on our right and the green slope to our left. In recent years, summer houses have begun to appear at the foot of the mountain: four or five wood-brown humps in a field of green. At a glance they all look the same, except for the one that stood here before this cottage community; it is abandoned and run down and has been since I first came here more than ten years ago.

In the car, the last song on the Cream album is barely audible. When the radio cut out in the last valley I put the CD on, just to hear the song 'White Room'. A few years ago I reclaimed a portion of my vinyl collection in the form of anthologies of Cream, Led Zeppelin, Deep Purple, and Jethro Tull. I'd ditched my LPs ages ago; a lot of them had actually been scratched to death at secondary school parties in the seventies. I enjoy running through the lyrics to 'White Room' in my mind: a song about a white room with black curtains near a railroad station. It sounds depressing and artistic and makes me feel like I'm alone, young, and independent in an empty room where the future is a snow white, blank page.

Our younger daughter is sleeping in the back seat,

the elder is still whining, 'When are we gonna get there, when are we gonna get there?' Erna tells her happily that the journey is as good as over. The level of irritation in the car peaked just before the middle of the trip, and the second half has been tolerable. The girls have been fighting over hair-slides and chewing gum and whether the elder had been poking the younger or not. Erna always keeps her cool with the girls and is rarely harsh with them. I, on the other hand, yell at them every time I lose my patience, which is pretty often. Then Erna scolds me, and if I return the favour the eruption can be a loud one. Today it happened shortly after we passed Varmahlíð in Skagafjörður. Erna ordered me to stop, jumped out of the car, and marched off onto the moors. I ran after her, chased her down and, even though I was furious, managed to force out some sort of conditional apology. No more was needed; the desire for reconciliation shone in her teary eyes.

When we drive into the village, it's an entirely different and much larger place than the picture it presented from behind the ridge. From there you can only see the old town centre, but in the hills beyond there are a number of single-family homes of varying sizes from the past few decades.

We always stay on the main street, though, in the basement of the bankers' house. Erna's brother is the branch manager of the Agricultural Bank and lives with his family in this old stone building next to the bank. They occupy the ground floor and the attic, while the basement is used for guest rooms and storage. For months at a time, nobody enters the basement, but when we're expected Erna's sister-in-law scrubs the floors and dusts the walls and windowsills.

But she never touches the stuff in the store room. There I immerse myself in copies of *Úrval* magazine from 1950 to 1973. The oldest issues contain speculations about future lunar missions, but the newest ones feature articles about large computers that fill 20-square-metre rooms and instructions on how to smoke a pipe. There's also a stack of old copies of *The Week*. One issue, from 1977, contains an interview with a young student from the countryside who lives in the old university dormitory. He says he can make ends meet pretty comfortably with his student loans, especially when his summer earnings are added to the mix. I read this article last year, too, and the year before that, but now I realise that the student is my boss at my new job, the project manager at the ad agency. He's long-haired and bearded in the picture, but his eyes and nose are instantly recognisable, and the name removes any shadow of a doubt, even though he's clean-shaven and cuts his hair short nowadays. At the time of this interview, I had started secondary school, begun listening to loud rock music and writing poetry.

There's also a decent collection of vinyl records there, and in an otherwise empty room straight across from the bathroom stands an old stereo with a glass-lidded turntable. The record collection includes a live recording of Cream's 'White Room', the song I was listening to in the car on the way over. The live recording is more fun, more energetic, the guitar solo at the end is longer. When my brother-in-law and his wife are at work and Erna has taken the girls out for a walk that I've somehow managed to avoid, I put the record on and leave the doors to both the room and the bathroom wide open as I take a shower, the pulsating music mingling with the sound of rushing water. In the shower I start thinking about vodka and Coke; the water of the shower tastes almost like this drink that probably hasn't passed my lips since the early 1980s.

By the time I've dried myself and dressed it's almost as if I've got a hangover from the memory of vodka, or rather as if it's just past noon on a 1978 Saturday again. I'm getting over a late night at the City Hotel and listening to this song, 'White Room', in my bedroom, singing both the lyrics and the guitar riff along with Clapton. Playing the song over and over again. I'm in a downright foul mood because a girl that I'd been thinking of dating pretty much ignored me the whole night before, and to make matters worse, my friend - or a cretin who called himself my friend - danced far too long and intimately with her. I headed straight home from the party at about two in the morning without saying goodbye to anyone. Gradually the song morphs my unbearable misery into tolerably romantic self-pity. I get really into the performance. The singing is powerful and entirely stripped of sentimentality, but the song and the performance are tragic all the same; somewhere in the audience is the girl from last night, listening and watching me on the stage.

After six or seven repetitions I was feeling well enough to go watch the replay of last week's English football match, which was about to start playing on TV. But when I stepped out, Dad was standing outside my door with a wide, mocking grin on his face. 'I think you need to feed your cows. The mooing in the barn is getting awfully loud.' I was used to clenching my teeth and silently enduring dad's shots at my taste in music, but this time I was in too bad a mood to keep a lid on it and spat out without thinking, 'Better than you!'

Dad's face was one big question mark for a moment before a self-satisfied smirk settled across his features. 'Better than me? What's the meaning of this nugget of wisdom?'

'It's just better than you.' My voice was shaking, I swallowed saliva, and my heart was thumping. 'It's not like you know how to play or anything. This is one of the best guitar players in the world and not some mooing cow.'

Dad burst out laughing. 'Yeah, don't spare your praise for the screaming banshees, son, you don't need to rein it in for my sake.' He walked away laughing, but I muttered after him: 'I think people shouldn't mouth off if they don't know the first thing about music.' My heart was still pounding in my chest.

Dad was 56 years old when I was born, and by the time I was in secondary school he had quit working. My siblings were the same age as my friends' parents, but my dad was like an ancient visitor to me. A peculiar, sarcastic man who lives with the family but is none of your business. And still, there lingered some unclear memory of the warmth in his embrace, but that memory seemed to be of a different man, long gone. I had once written a warm greeting to that man with a blue crayon on a light grey sheet of wrapping paper. He corrected me kindly: I had written 'datty' instead of 'daddy'. The mistake was etched in my mind, and for several years afterwards, I would remember 'datty' and 'daddy' when I noticed spelling mistakes in my schoolwork. Gradually my awareness of words, sentences, paragraphs, and text grew. Spelling and creative writing became my strongest subjects, and in secondary school I began entertaining dreams of becoming a poet, complete with prose poems, self-important company, café hangouts, a green army surplus jacket, a beret, long trench coats, colourful scarves and neckties.

Reality, on the other hand, would have me be a proofreader. An excellent proofreader, as it happened. And it's here in this basement that the memories rush forth, in a place that has nothing to do with my past.

On every visit here, we are invited to Hannes and Fríða's for a barbecue. They live in a little house up in the hills behind the town centre. The ocean is still and pale blue this evening, and from here the heathered mountain slopes on the other side of the fjord seem much closer than they do from the town centre, even though I'm farther away from them here. There appears to be a hint of evening red in the light that illuminates the fjord, but that can hardly be the case; it isn't even seven o'clock on a July evening.

At the end of this gravel road, a stone's throw from their house, is a mechanic's garage. Outside the garage building there are car carcasses propped up on their wings and two intact Volkswagen Golfs. I've never seen people around the garage, since I only come here on a weekend evening once each summer, and so this scene always leaves me with the impression that nothing has been done here for many years.

Fríða and Erna are childhood friends, but Hannes is an outsider whom Fríða met when they were about twenty. Fríða is sincere, open and chatty, argumentative with Hannes, who is quiet and grave. When Fríða gives him a hard time in front of us he always responds in exactly the same way: says nothing in response but sighs heavily.

Erna and Fríða embrace each other, and a moment later Fríða shakes my hand warmly and says: 'Welcome! It's wonderful to see you.' People don't greet each other this way in Reykjavík, I think with affection. Fríða is fairly big-boned and looks a few years older than she is. Her eyes are large and dark, and when she meets your gaze, they seem laden with sorrow and sympathy, even though they really aren't.

Hannes is opening a bottle of red wine in the living room. 'Nice to see you again,' says Erna and proffers a hand; Hannes shakes it silently and blushes. He responds to my greeting with a mumble.

We sit for a while in the living room and sip at the red wine. Fríða asks us about the trip, but Hannes remains silent. Their younger son, who had an ear infection last year and lay screaming in his bed while we ate, comes barrelling into the room and sweeps a bunch of loose objects off the table, right in front of the chair where Hannes is sitting. Among the casualties is my glass of red wine, and I get a bit of a splash on my pants, while Hannes' good fortune is that he is holding his glass. Fríða lets out a shout, darts into the kitchen to fetch a wet rag, wipes me down, cleans the floor and picks up the shards of glass, all in the blink of an eye.

She glares at Hannes: 'Are you fast asleep, man, or is it only my responsibility to watch the boy!' Hannes doesn't answer, just lets out a weighty sigh. Then he stands up, picks up the boy, and says: 'Let's get the grill started.' I stand up as well, since I feel like I would be better off at the grill than alone with the women in the living room. But Hannes doesn't take the boy out the back door to the grill, but rather into the playroom. The elder boy can be heard howling about the visit, and within minutes the younger has left the room again. I peek through the door and see the older boy sitting at a game console. He is skinny with a light red head of hair and a grumpy expression. He has become nearly unrecognisable since the last time I saw him; children change fast.

My daughters are in the backyard, playing with three cats that curl up in the uncut grass and jump up onto a fence and back down again from time to time. The girls beg a package of ham from Fríða in the kitchen, where she and Erna have begun preparing a salad and dressings. The girls divide the slices of ham among the cats, who chew on them in a leisurely fashion. The younger son runs towards them and falls in the grass. Two of the cats leap away, fleeing, but the third saunters off from the grassy patch with the slice of ham in his mouth and lays it on the gravel in the driveway.

The girls start playing with the boy, making him a crown of dandelions, buttercups, and daffodils. He runs in joyous circles in the grass, wearing his crown, and the girls shriek.

Hannes brings out two platters, piled high with steaks and sausages, and two white bowls, one with seasoning and one with foil-wrapped potatoes; he places them on a table next to the grill. He offers me a beer and fetches two cans of green Tuborg. He lights up a cigarette and lets it dangle from the corner of his mouth while he begins preparing the food; lights up the grill, seasons the meat.

The flavour of the canned beer evokes a feeling of emptiness, not because I dislike beer, but because there's something about it that makes me feel that existence is bland.

Hannes works silently at the grill, and I try to think of something to say. Fríða and Erna's constant chatter in the kitchen carries out to us, punctuated with laughter. Even though I don't particularly want to talk to Hannes and know that he doesn't mind the silence at all, it makes me somehow uncomfortable. In my mind I try to develop some interest in the cooking, and I'm about to ask some question about the seasoning he's using when Fríða suddenly appears in the doorway and says: 'Good Lord, how much you smoke, man.' Hannes doesn't answer, but takes the cigarette out of his mouth and sighs heavily. Fríða smiles and lets loose a long mumble to express her satisfaction with the smell from the grill. Hannes tosses the half-smoked cigarette away, but the instant that Fríða disappears from the doorway he lights up another.

My seasoning question has become outdated in some inexplicable way, since I wasn't able to get it out earlier. So I ask how the weather's been this summer. Hannes doesn't answer at first, but then he says there was a 'goddamned fog' in the fjord for most of June, but July's been all right so far. I ask whether they barbecue often, and my mouth feels numb from boredom over asking about these things that I have no interest in. Hannes answers with a sort of smacking of his lips or clicking of the tongue that probably is meant to indicate that the answer is up for debate.

After another long silence he suddenly asks me where I'm working nowadays. I tell him that I've just started working as a proofreader at an ad agency.

'Weren't you a journalist? At *Morgunblaðið*?' I tell him that I was a copy editor when I worked at *Mogginn*, not a journalist. As if having heard nothing I said, he says he's stopped reading the papers, has terminated his subscriptions to both *Morgunblaðið* and *DV*. The TV is plenty.

A moment later he asks me to take the first batch of meat and sausages inside. Fríða and Erna have set the table. The younger son waddles around the room with a cat in his arms. He trips in the dining room, the cat escapes his prison and jumps up on the table. Erna and Fríða both shriek, and Fríða shoos at the cat, who flees outside without any food. I fetch the potatoes.

Hannes keeps grilling for a good while after we've sat down. When he finally comes inside he's clearly starving and tears into the food. He serves himself seconds before any of us have finished our first serving, even though we started long before him. Unless my eyes are playing tricks on me, he's put on quite a bit of weight since last year, and he was no waif to begin with. It seems like Hannes has always been fat, but that's not true: in photos from the oldest barbecues he's pretty average. But he's kept expanding steadily, year by year.

Though I'm sure it's not fun being fat, there's something that I envy about Hannes' greed. I was starving hungry myself when we sat down, but after a few bites the same feeling overwhelms me as with the beer earlier: life is bland.

I do better with the dessert, Fríða's homemade ice cream; the sugar rushes to my head and lets a fresh breeze into my mind for a brief moment. But Hannes has finished two bowls before I'm through with my one. He gets up with the empty bowl, probably to have a third helping, just as Fríða storms in from the kitchen and says: 'I found five cigarette butts on the porch where you left them! What a filthy mess!' Hannes sits back down and heaves a sigh.

The children go back out to play after dinner, our daughters and their younger son, but the elder boy comes out with his socks dangling from his feet and nibbles at a piece of meat while standing up. Then he takes a bowl of ice cream into the playroom.

Erna and Fríða lose themselves in chit-chat about girls they went to school with, who is where, who married and who divorced. Hannes and I sit across from each other, me in the sofa next to Erna, he in his chair, and seem doomed to remain silent while the women natter away. But suddenly Erna mentions the summer houses on the slope outside the town, says that there seem to be more of them. This makes Hannes come alive; his face brightens as if a curtain has been drawn back in a dark room. Fríða says that they've been toying with the idea of building a cottage but that it's just so expensive. She sighs and looks dreamily off into the distance.

'It doesn't have to be so terribly expensive,' says Hannes

and gets up. There is life in the lumbering body now, and he shifts his weight from one foot to the other in front of the sofa and then starts pacing the floor. 'You know that Sigga and Bjartur are interested in this. Two couples, even three, can join forces and do it together. You can get Norwegian and Finnish houses with all the materials prepared, which is more expensive of course, but if people are willing to work at it a bit and do it as a team, you can put up a house for three million. That's a million and a half per couple. That's like buying a car.'

'I really dislike taking big loans, and we really could do with replacing the car,' says Fríða. I get the feeling that this is well trodden ground. Despite the eagerness in Hannes' voice, there's an undertone of mechanical repetition.

'And we don't have any savings,' says Fríða.

'We can start saving now,' Hannes replies. And now it's Fríða who sighs, not him. Her facial expression seems to indicate that she thinks Hannes has earned her cooperation on this one, or that she actually wants to play along, but still doesn't trust herself to do it. She says it would be lovely to spend summer weekends and days off on the grassy slopes of the mountain and let the boys play outside in natural surroundings. Hannes rattles off figures for the cost of materials and labour. His eyes shine. I myself can't see any difference between a peaceful village and a hillside just outside the town. All I know is that there's much less space in a summer house than a regular family home.

Erna says that she thinks it would be a bit too much to build or buy a cottage for several million, but she would love to be able to rent one for a week or so each summer. But you just can't get in anywhere, the union-owned houses are always booked up long in advance.

I envision a large cluster of summer houses in a wide expanse of uniform vegetation that has all been planted in a reforestation effort. The cottages all look the same: small and wood-brown. It rains all the time, and the heavy, cloud-grey sky envelops the greenish-brown flatness. The summer house is cramped, and there is no peace to be had for reading or thinking about useless and vague things. The girls are constantly trudging in water and mud from the rain-saturated fields, and Erna follows them with a mop in silent irritation. The girls argue constantly, I bellow at them, and Erna hisses at me. She drags us all outside on long walks, and we march about the area in long raincoats, look at the planted saplings and the brown summer houses. At night there is drinking in the neighbouring cottages and I lie awake, more out of envy than due to the noise. My envy doesn't stem from a desire to join them – I can hardly imagine anything worse – but from the knowledge that someone is having such a good time while I count the days, hours, minutes, and seconds until I get back home.

On the other hand, I did have a daydream long ago that was related to a summer house. It was after I had started dating Erna, but before the girls were born. I saw myself struggling to finish the manuscript for a novel. The publisher is putting a great deal of pressure on me to get it out before Christmas, since my last novel sold extremely well. As a result, I've decided to shut myself up in a summer house that Erna and I bought with the royalties from the last book. Our cottage is situated in a sheltered valley, and there is sunshine and a gentle breeze most of the time. I sit outside at a table in the lovely weather and hammer away at a school typewriter. On the table is a stack of typed pages. Erna visits me from time to time, though she tries very hard to interrupt my work as little as possible. Our children are with her, but I can't make out their number, gender, or age. Yet I seem to recall that some versions of the daydream feature a mature and intelligent boy who takes strongly after me. The boy is a great bookworm. He's going to be a writer like his dad when he grows up.

July 1999

Quite a shock awaits me in the basement of the bankers' house: the storage rooms have been emptied. For the last hour of the drive I hardly thought about anything but the old magazines and LPs, while moors, mountains and fields with hay bales shrink-wrapped in white plastic sped past the car windows, an endless and unchanging road ahead until I spied the town just beyond the hill.

The old stereo has vanished, too. That room has been filled with a TV and a game console, and on the floor is a box, crammed full of toy cars and plastic soldiers.

I ask my brother-in-law about this, and he says he drove all the stuff to the dump this winter. 'It was time to get rid of all that junk.' He says there are new copies of *Mannlíf* magazine on his desk that I'm welcome to read. And I can play music in the living room whenever I like. He has some new CDs by U2 and Sálin.

I go back down to the basement and lie down on the bed in the guest bedroom. Booted feet walk past the window. I hear the screeching of a truck. Then all is quiet. In this basement I would relive the past because the magazines and records evoked memories of old times. But even now, when I have no such tangible objects, I still start thinking about the past – an old habit linked to this basement.

When I was 12 or 13 years old an older cousin of mine invited me to see an age-restricted film at Tónabíó theatre, where a friend of his was working as a doorman for the summer. I was really excited about it, having never seen a film rated 16-and-over; only a few 12-and-overs and one 14-and-over. I had longed, without the least morsel of hope, to get to see this film, because it wasn't just age-restricted; the advertisement in *Mogginn* said: *Strictly prohibited for children under 16 years of age. Identification required.*

Dad happened upon us in the kitchen as we were

talking about the film with the *Mogginn* movie pages open in front of us on the kitchen table. He had just stepped in from a walk, with his flat cap still on and holding the light brown cane he sometimes used even though he wasn't the least bit lame. He was wearing a worn grey suit and a wool sweater under the jacket; a north wind was blowing that evening, sunny but cool.

'Are you really going to waste your time gaping at murder and violent abuse in a cinema?' Dad crowed. My cousin protested: 'What, it's a real thriller, man.' Dad cursed and scolded, raised up his cane and shouted: 'You'll see, boys, nothing good will come of amusing the devil!' His eyes were dark with anger and the corner of his mouth shook. I suspected that he'd had an argument in the neighbourhood, and that the anger from that was still erupting.

I had no recollection of Dad's ever forbidding me to do anything. He expressed disapproval of my intentions and interests in an impersonal way, as if I were irrelevant to him, just a part of the nameless youth and the spirit of the times.

When I came home from the theatre that night, my cat had vanished. More precisely, he hadn't come home in three days. I had expected him home that night; he took off every so often, but always came back on the second or third day. Until now, that is: I never saw him again after that. For a long time afterward, I was to miss having him snuggle at the foot of my bed, and I was never fully able to erase the thought from my mind that I had lost him because I got into the age-restricted film at Tónabíó. In some ways, that mental block stemmed from my deep-seated belief that Dad was always right, even though I never paid him any attention on the surface of it. His prophetic words in the kitchen that night echoed in my mind every time I thought of my cat from then on.

But I had also developed this notion that there was some cosmic balance between good and bad fortune in life, which had caused what seemed too good to be true to be exactly that. I had snuck in to the 16-rated film and lost the cat as a result. In a way I had chosen between the film and the cat, and of course I'd made the wrong choice.

Erna's sister-in-law is the custodian at the new sports centre. One evening she offers us the use of the sauna. We leave the girls behind. It's strange to be in a brand new building in this old, familiar town. The building seems mostly empty, but when I step into the men's locker room there are clothes on almost every hook, and the floor is half-covered with duffel bags. On one of the hooks a dark grey suit hangs on a hanger. The breast pocket is adorned with a large and colourful logo. When I look closer I see that it's the emblem of the FAI, the Football Association of Iceland. Suddenly I hear the whoosh of a kicked ball followed by a referee's whistle.

Erna and I sit naked and silent in the sauna, but it's a pleasant silence; a rare moment of peace. Suddenly no children, no usual topics of conversation like pending chores, apartment maintenance, car inspections, oil changes, car washes, to-do lists for tomorrow, parent-teacher conferences, ballet lessons, gymnastics lessons, recorder concerts. Suddenly it's all evaporated with the hot steam, and time has ceased to exist. Of course we don't have anything to talk about in such a rare instant of tranquillity; instead, we enjoy relaxing together in silence.

I look at Erna: the steam obscures the bits of wear and tear that age has begun to leave on her body and smoothes out her face. But her naked body awakens no lust in me. I call an image of her to my mind as she was when she was young and I was in love with her. But I feel like I wouldn't fall in love with that girl if I met her now because I'm not the same person I was. I've outlived romantic love before the age of forty.

Suddenly Erna becomes aware that I'm looking at her, meets my eyes, in surprise at first but then she smiles tenderly. I break the silence and say that we should probably go shower or at least get our towels, since there's no telling when the football match might be over. As I say these words, I find myself gripped by a vestige of an old excitement, a hint of tension.

Erna yelps and asks angrily why I didn't tell her that there was a game in progress. She throws the door open and storms out.

Hannes and Fríða have made their dreams of a summer house a reality, and this time they have us over for a barbecue in their newly built wood-panelled summer house on the slope above the town. I inch the car up a steep and rocky trail. The wheels spin and send pebbles and sand flying, and I send up silent thanks for the brightness of summer evenings.

An incomprehensible and unpleasant sense of surprise latches on to me as we step out of the car. As if something isn't as it should be. Fríða and Hannes are standing on the veranda and smiling at us. They have their arms around each other. I can't recall seeing them touch each other before, at least not since 1990. Hannes is thin. I swear, he must have lost about sixty pounds. For a brief moment I feel like I'm shaking off a dream after an accidental nap: Hannes looking thin, Hannes smiling with an arm around Fríða. What is going on here?

The main difference between eating barbecued meat in a summer cottage and a house is the lack of space. We sit around a small, round plastic table with hardly enough space for our plates. Thank goodness the kids prefer to eat out on the veranda, where they nibble at hot dogs and hamburgers.

Though I feel like it's effeminate and silly to talk about weight loss regimes, I'm curious enough to ask Hannes what sort of a programme he went through to lose the weight. He shakes his head, mumbles, tosses up a hand: 'M-m, no weight loss programme, none of that crap.' He says he eats exactly the same food as he did before, just much less. Says he makes sure to stop eating before he feels full, because he always ends up feeling sated a short while later. 'I just stopped being so goddamned greedy,' he ends his succinct speech.

Erna and Fríða lend their enthusiastic support, and I nod, as it certainly sounds very reasonable. It's not like I know anything about obesity, but I wonder why fat people don't lose weight sooner if it's so easy. I couldn't suddenly become greedy just by deciding to. Can the greedy suddenly just decide to have less of an appetite? It occurs to me that Hannes may have been so happy to get the summer house that it weaned him from his overeating, and as armchair psychology goes, it seems no worse a theory than any other.

Hannes still eats as fast as he ever did, but after a little while he pushes the plate with his half-eaten cutlet away with a sour expression on his face, and for a brief moment a familiar heaviness shades his features, otherwise conspicuously absent this evening. But he cheers up again soon enough and adopts a dreamy look.

After dinner, Hannes and Fríða sit down side-by-side on a plaid sofa, while Erna and I drag chairs from the plastic table over to the coffee table. They sit close together, hold hands, let go, caress each other's hands. It's almost as if they had just met a few weeks ago.

There is something familiar about this plaid sofa, and I eventually realise that it was in their living room many years ago, at the first barbecues. In the window by the kitchen nook, among the dead flies, is an old radio that also looks familiar.

Fríða stares admiringly at Hannes, but he is absent-minded and distant, and although he squeezes her hand it's more as if he accepts her affection than reciprocates it. He rises to his feet, knocks on the walls, admires the wood, says the material is of excellent quality but was still reasonably priced; he raps on the windows, which he says are double glazed and from Íspan. Fríða's eyes follow his every movement, and her outstretched hand waits for him when he sits back down on the sofa, twines with his, presses eagerly.

The kids are playing outside, and their shouts float in through the open door from time to time. It's cloudy but dry, and the evening breeze is warm even though there's a hint of fog on the moor to the south. I pop out to see the kids. I want to chat with my girls about something mundane and timeless, something sufficiently unrelated to this strange change that has been wrought in our hosts. But the kids are busy playing tag in circles around the cottage and can't be bothered to talk to me. The game seems to be to have the younger son chase everyone else; he always seems to be the one who's 'it'.

I look out across the fjord. The sea is grey-blue and a bit choppy, even though the weather is warm. Hannes and Fríða's sudden bliss awakes in me a strange apprehension that churns in the waves.

When I go back inside, Fríða is praising Sigga and Bjartur, the couple who built the summer house with them. How dependable and diligent they are, how they held up their end of the bargain, what good companions they are. The two families even spent a weekend together in the house and no one suffered from the lack of space.

Hannes doesn't say a word on this score, doesn't even nod. Instead he draws out a crumpled pack of cigarettes, puts one in his mouth, and lights up with a green lighter from a sweetshop. Fríða gets up, goes into the kitchen and opens a cabinet above the microwave. A moment later she places a small clear ashtray on the coffee table. I meet Erna's eyes in surprise, but she looks away and pretends nothing has happened.

When Erna and I went to bed the night after our return to Reykjavík, a long conversation took place, a conversation that I had dreaded without fully realising it. Erna said she had been surprised and thrilled at the change in Hannes and Fríða. But it also prompted her to reflect seriously on our relationship. Because it simply couldn't go on like this anymore. We never talked to each other and I always seemed to be thinking about something other than her, the girls, and the household. And yet she had no idea where I dwelled in my mind, because I seemed to have no interest in anything except playing old rock albums and leafing through books and magazines. To make matters worse, we were constantly arguing because I had trouble controlling my temper and wasn't sensitive enough with the girls. I said I thought the girls were getting along just fine.

'No thanks to you,' she retorted. 'You seem to have no interest in your children or your wife.' I said that I had found Fríða and Hannes really strange that night, almost disturbing. She said that I clearly didn't want to discuss these matters seriously, since I was trying to be funny about it. I said that I couldn't recall her ever having been critical of Hannes and Fríða's relationship before, at least not in my presence, and that I had always thought they had a perfectly normal marriage, just like ours. I was having a hard time understanding why they had suddenly turned into lovesick teenagers and doubted that a summer house could bring about such a sea change in our relationship.

Erna said she didn't have a summer house in mind, but a marriage counsellor, a course at some church down in Suðurnes and a couples' retreat at Þingvellir. I stiffened in silent terror and gave no reply.

October 1999

One evening I'm pottering around in the basement at home; Erna has sent me down there with an old kitchen stool covered in dried splotches of paint. I rummage around in boxes of books, checking for old titles that I might want to read again.

In one of the boxes I stumble upon old notebooks that I thought we'd thrown out years ago. They mostly contain my own poems and failed drafts of short stories. In a fit of masochistic curiosity I scan through a few pages, and the text seems even worse than I could have imagined. Yet I know I can't judge it with the least bit of fairness, having proclaimed my verdict long ago. As a teenager I enjoyed publishing poetic pretensions of greatness in the school newspapers and showing off among friends at cafés. But after my secondary school diploma, the dream took a serious turn and I stayed awake long into the night composing short stories. By day I was studying Icelandic at the University. I had no experience of life, and so the stories weren't about anything, but I struggled hard to write well about nothing.

I had turned 24 years old when I took my best story to a meeting with the editor of *Mál og Menning Magazine*. I had actually made the same journey with another story two years earlier but run into an acquaintance outside Mál og Menning's publishing house on Laugavegur and struck up a conversation with him. It was then I realised that my voice was quivering, I was so nervous. My acquaintance asked what was the matter, and I realised that if I couldn't control my voice while talking about pop culture with him, I would hardly be able to stay standing in front of the editor.

But on the same mission two years later, with a different and polished story in my hands, I wasn't nervous at all. Granted, I didn't particularly like the story, but I didn't consider that much of a disadvantage, given some of the other things I'd read in the magazine. The story seemed well structured, and I could even analyse it myself according to the principles of literary analysis.

The editor was a friendly fellow of about forty - a nationally recognised poet - in jeans and a worn sweater. He gave a friendly greeting, offered me coffee, and took his time reading the story while I sat across from him in front of the desk.

The story was five typewritten pages, and after about ten minutes the editor looked up from the manuscript, smiled, and said that the story wasn't good enough for the magazine. 'Go home and keep writing,' he said.

I went home but did not keep writing. Dad had died two years earlier, but now I saw him shouting after me down Bankastræti: 'What is the meaning of this nonsense, boy? Just wait and see, no good will come of this writing business!'

And yet I don't really have any idea what Dad would have thought of my being a writer. His disapproval was always aimed at boyish pursuits: fireworks, climbing up half-finished buildings, rock music, thriller films. But I didn't need a father now; I had the editor.

When I come up from the basement, the notebooks hover in my darkened mind, and I realise that it doesn't matter whether I throw them away or not; I'll never be completely free of them.

The phone rings and I answer. A friendly female voice greets me with kindness: 'Good to hear your voice, Bjarni!' She asks how we are all doing. I can't quite place the voice but know I'm supposed to know her, so I try not to give anything away but answer the woman hesitantly. She asks how the weather is at our end, and I tell her it's rainy and windy. The woman says she's had more than enough of the fog that's enveloped the fjord for weeks on end. Then I realise it's Fríða on the line. At that very moment she asks for Erna.

When I have handed Erna the receiver, I suddenly feel at a loose end, as if I'm not used to doing anything other than talking on the phone in the evenings and don't know what to do with myself without it. I hesitate for a moment but then move towards my elder daughter's room. The door is open, and she's sitting in a white nightdress at her little desk, completely immersed in her drawing. It sounds like Erna and Fríða are waxing critical about some people in the town, as they often do. One of the husbands has crossed the line, by the sound of it. Maybe a drinker, as there seem to be many of those around, though I've never actually seen one in the throes of intoxication; it's as if they all shut themselves indoors in the summer only to flood out into the streets in autumn and set the town ablaze.

I have hardly thought about Hannes and Fríða since we came back from this summer's trip, but now I suddenly feel like they haven't left Erna's and my side for a single day. Their presence reveals itself in the fact that we have yet to have an argument since that summer vacation. Not even one. The conversation we had the night after the trip steps silently forward every time one of us is about to run out of patience.

I watch my daughter draw and listen to my wife as she talks on the phone. But I can't see what my daughter is drawing and I can't hear what my wife is saying. I can just see a few lines on the page and catch bits and pieces of Erna's conversation, with no real chance of holding it in my mind.

'Has the man gone out of his skull?' says Erna. She would never talk this way about me. Men who do what they please get described like this in women's conversations. The ones who are more obedient, men like me, who don't leave their families, don't get drunk, and don't cheat, but are otherwise not particularly good husbands, men who are too spineless to be either good or bad – the women talk *at* us like this but not *about* us. 'Have you gone crazy? Did you forget to empty the washing machine? What on Earth made you dress the child in pants with holes in them? Can you never finish anything? Are you going to watch TV the whole weekend? Have you lost your mind?'

I want to talk to my daughter, about what I don't know. But she's fully absorbed in her drawing and hardly interested in being interrupted. Sometimes she's desperate to talk to me, to tell me something thoroughly remarkable, but at such times I'm usually indisposed. I don't have the faintest recollection of why I have so little time for her; that gets forgotten right away. I tiptoe into her room and sit quietly on her bed. She doesn't seem to notice me. I look at her back, how her shoulders shift up and down as she uses the pencil. Long, dark hair, white nightdress. I listen to her breathing, how she grunts in concentration. When she was an infant I sometimes fed her milk from a baby bottle on the sofa. She sat in my lap, her back towards me, wearing a babygrow held together by poppers, gulped down the milk and I could feel how her little stomach swelled under my fingertips. She's a completely different person now and will be unrecognisable again in a few years.

In front of me hang a number of drawings of hers, affixed to the wall with Blu-Tack. Most of them are fair-featured princesses with long tresses, full lips, and large almond-shaped eyes. But one of the pictures is different. It clearly depicts the barbecue at Hannes and Fríða's this summer. Yet a variety of liberties have been taken with the facts. We are all standing on the veranda, and she's the one doing the grilling. Hannes is fat in the picture, though he was thin this summer. He has a cigarette in his mouth, which is giving off a lot of smoke. His younger son stands by the grill and waits for a slice from the grill master. She has drawn a speech bubble above her head and written in it: 'Enjoy your dinner!'

I have long ago stopped expecting any surprises in life, either good or bad, and at any rate I haven't the least suspicion that in fifteen minutes Erna will tell me that Hannes and Fríða are getting a divorce. But if I were to go out front and listen properly, I could figure it out right now.

She calls me into the living room after the phone call. At that point our daughter has finished her drawing, climbed into bed, and pulled up the duvet. She lets out a heartfelt yawn, not a care in the world, and falls asleep almost immediately. Erna asks me to sit down on the sofa with her, where she usually naps in the evening while I watch TV or rifle through books and magazines. But this time we are both wide awake, if numb with shock. Hannes apparently first asked for a divorce last winter. He had a number of complaints, many things he had kept silent about for a long time, stayed quiet and sighed heavily. Constant nagging and inconstant sex, for instance. And above all, Fríða's hesitance at moving forward with the summer house investment.

After a few tense hours of tears and fury, Fríða swallowed her pride and said that she was prepared to better herself if Hannes would reconsider his decision. He agreed, and what followed were several months of renewed affections that probably peaked around the time we visited last summer.

But as summer turned to fall, Hannes became severe, silent, and distant. Fríða asked what was the matter, whether he was anxious about the coming winter and not being able to spend as much time in the summer house as before. Then Hannes threw his hands in the air and shouted that he couldn't play along any more. This was just impossible, and they had to get divorced. When asked whether he had really been acting out his happiness all this time, he replied that he had acted so well he even had himself convinced. But the truth was that love either lived or it didn't, and there was nothing anyone could do about it. He realised now that it wasn't about nagging or affection, good sex or no sex, a summer house or no summer house. As strange as that might sound. She had really done a great job, there was nothing to find fault with in her anymore, and there were many good things in their life, but the spark was missing. At the end of the day, it wasn't about her, but about him. He was unhappy with himself, tired of himself, wanted to start over, maybe move away and go to college. He would have to start a new life, because he was losing the will to live.

Yesterday Fríða had found a suspicious text message on his mobile. It was inappropriately affectionate and was from a woman in the town, the very same Sigga who had joined them in building the summer house along with her husband. Fríða had yet to confront him about it, but she didn't really see the point in it anymore. She was completely miserable over the whole thing and didn't know which way to turn.

'This is what can happen when people don't cultivate their relationship,' Erna says and shoots a nervous glance my way. I wonder if she's serious.

'No, this is what can happen when someone goes crazy,' I say and snort out a joyless laugh.

'Right you are,' Erna agrees and laughs as well for an instant. 'But he said the love was gone.'

'What is love?' I reply and snort again, this time without laughter.

'Exactly,' Erna says and the frozen terror in her face thaws a little. I don't know where this sudden gift for words comes from, but nevertheless I seem to have hit a train of thought that I sense is to Erna's liking. It's been a long time since I've said something that meets with her approval, and it's a good feeling.

'Love and happiness, isn't it just a question of choice, isn't it just something that people decide?' I finish, and Erna nods slowly and determinedly.

When we go to bed I'm afraid that Erna will pick up our conversation about couples' weekend church retreats and the like. She wouldn't want us to go the way of Hannes and Fríða, after all. But now my position is strengthened in this regard, and I'm determined to remind her that she used their purported marital bliss to justify the same plans this summer.

But Erna says nothing in bed. She wraps her arms around me, holds me tight, loosens her grip for a brief moment and gives me a nudge to indicate that I should embrace her more tightly. I obey her and immediately feel an erection developing, know that she's not looking for that right now, any more than usual, and keep myself under control.

After a long while, Erna lets go, kisses my cheek good night, and rolls over on her other side.

Something that Hannes supposedly said to Fríða rings a bell in my mind and seems connected to an old memory. It was the bit about the lack of a spark. After long reflection I realise what the memory is: it's connected with the erstwhile editor of *Mál og Menning Magazine*. Suddenly I recall what it was exactly that he said about my story. Not just that it wasn't good enough for the magazine. Now I remember that he said it was well written but lacked spark. Yes, he said, 'This is well done but lacks spark.' Maybe he said something else, something that was supposed to be encouraging, but I paid no attention, paralysed by disappointment and shame.

'Well done but lacks spark,' I repeat a few times in my mind and move my lips in a soundless mutter. For some reason, perhaps because I'm on the verge of falling asleep, it doesn't sound too bad to me. Still, the sentence seems to need some improvement, and the very next moment I find the solution. I change the word order: 'Lacks spark, but well done.' I say it over a few times. It really doesn't sound bad at all. Maybe it doesn't sound very good either, but it's enough for me as I drift off to sleep.

A Sweet Shop in the West End

IT USED TO be one of the grocery shops run by the Retailers'
Cooperative of Greater Reykjavík - RCGR. Nowadays
the old meat counter serves as a video rental, and racks of
videotapes take up a large portion of the floor space. In front
of the video area are a few groceries in shelves and coolers.
Behind the counter the traditional sweet shop fare and
lottery tickets are kept. By the wall next to the entrance are
two slot machines.

The shop has looked more or less like this since the
mid-eighties. The inventory is kept in the basement as
before. There used to be a coffee nook there too, but now
it's on the ground floor, back behind the register.

Next door there used to be a milk shop, but it's
been replaced by a fishmonger's shop. There used to be
a fishmonger two doors down, but now it's a firearms
dealership and repair shop. From 1989 to 1999 it had housed
a shoemaker.

One day in July 1970, a delivery truck driver came here
with a boy just shy of eight years of age. The driver delivered
goods to the shop, and his young passenger was the son of
a woman he was seeing. The driver was married and his
relationship with the boy's mother far more loosely defined
than she would have liked. He came for coffee - sometimes
in the morning, but more commonly after dinner, and then
he usually stayed past midnight, long past the boy's bedtime.
Sometimes he wouldn't appear for a few weeks; sometimes

he was there night after night. She always tried to get him to stay the night, but he never indulged her wishes. Often it was just as if she were greeting her husband and the head of the household when he dropped in on her in the evenings: always prepared to heat up the leftovers from dinner (which he usually declined), offered him a seat in a tired-looking armchair in the living room, brought him a footrest and handed him a newspaper; then appeared moments later with a steaming cup of coffee, restless and excited in her servitude.

This morning she had begged the driver to take the boy along for the ride, and he had given in after a bit of quibbling. He had hardly ever paid the boy any attention, and so they were as good as strangers passing in the street. The boy was shy of the driver, even a little bit frightened of him. The driver's lack of interest was cold and forbidding but also prevented the fear from growing, because the driver never showed the slightest sign of wanting to interact with the boy.

On the other hand, the boy liked observing the driver, smelling his cologne, looking at the dark hairs on his strong arms and the plaid cotton shirts he wore, always with the sleeves rolled up. The boy enjoyed watching him smoke and put his wallet in his back pocket. This unassuming pantomime resonated with a vague recollection that failed to take shape in his mind.

The drive was exciting because the boy had very seldom even stepped into a car before. The driver did not deviate from habit and so didn't address him. At first the silence was heavy and awkward, but gradually the boy started studying the driver the same way he did in the kitchen and living room back home, watched him shift gears and move his feet on the pedals; inhaled the smell of aftershave infused with smoke.

Suddenly the boy needed to pee. When he worked up the nerve to tell the driver, they were approaching the RCGR shop, where they were going to deliver some goods. The driver took the boy into the shop, where the girl working the cash register walked him down to the toilet in the basement. The walls were bright red, and the light from a naked bulb made them seem wet and glistening. Below the mirror was a white sink, spotlessly cleaned. The entire bathroom was practically sterile, but it still seemed dirty because of the strange light created by the combination of the bulb and the colour of the walls.

A few days later the man's shaving kit caught the boy's eye in the bathroom at home. By then the driver had relented to repeated requests by the boy's mother that he shave at their place. The shaving kit reawakened the vague memory that had first surfaced when the boy observed the driver. But now it assumed a shape: he had seen a shaving kit in this bathroom before. He had long since forgotten it; it was so long ago and he had been so small. In a corner of his mind, a man in a vest appeared, his cheeks lathered with shaving soap. He smelled a cologne that was not inattentive but rather intimate, his face touched a man's cheek, and the smell of tobacco mingled with the cologne. He looked at buttercups and dandelions that had grown along a concrete wall. The sun's rays bounced off a blue engine hood, and he could smell grass. Then something like a dream: he is laid down in a big bed, and something white blocks his view; it is warm and protective. But when he wakes up it's gone and he's alone.

A Friday afternoon in late August 1991. The boy, a grown man now, nearly thirty. He was living up the hill in Breiðholt and rarely went to the West End, where he had grown up. He lived with a woman he had met a little over two years ago. The woman had a son from before, who was now four years old.

The man was on an aimless ride in his car with the stepson in the back seat. He had picked him up from the nursery school near their house, but he hadn't wanted to go straight home and instead opted to drive around a bit. Now he had himself going all the way down to the west part of town, to his childhood stamping grounds, without even thinking about it.

Earlier that day he'd been given a generous raise at the petrol station where he had worked as a cashier for the past few years: he'd been made store manager for the station. The joy should have been untainted, but he didn't want to tell the woman about it. On the other hand, he thought it would be ridiculous not to do it, and the tension was making him anxious. He wanted to have a partner who would be thrilled with the news of a promotion, but he dreaded her reaction. She might ask out of genuine curiosity how big a raise he would get; apart from that she would pretend to be thrilled and happy, and her false tone would grate on his ears.

If only he hadn't grown tired of going to the neighbourhood pub! He should have kept that to himself. Then everything would surely be as it ought to be. They had met at that pub back in the day, and for a long time they used to go there every weekend. The boy was with the woman's parents most weekends, a long-standing tradition. But the man began preferring to spend evenings resting in front of the TV. Ideally with the boy at home. Pop into his bedroom during commercial breaks and watch him sleep. Let his mind toy with the idea of a new child, an offspring of his own flesh and blood. Think about a new living room bookcase and sofa, or a new apartment with a second child's bedroom, preferably a terraced house.

The woman found these weekend doldrums terribly boring, and she constantly begged him to come with her to the pub. But he had grown tired of being there, suddenly found the noise intolerable, feeling exhausted after a week's work and frankly pretty immune to the beer, perhaps because he didn't really want to get drunk anymore. And everyone there was so hyper-tense with a careless joy that could morph at any moment into fury.

When she suggested that she go to the pub alone to meet her girlfriends, he agreed enthusiastically, glad to have her happy, relieved to be released from going. But before long she had begun going to the pub every weekend, sometimes on both Friday and Saturday evenings. Once in a while her girlfriends stopped by at their place and warmed up, doing their makeup all at once in the bathroom and maybe drinking one beer in the living room; all with the requisite chatter, bursts of laughter, and shrieks.

He liked these gatherings because they reminded him of when they first met. This was the group of girls he'd been lucky enough to run into, and he'd snagged the prettiest one among them. They were all young still, but every one of them was a single mother.

Soon he began to think it the lesser of two evils to go with her than to wait for her at home week after week, often not knowing what time she had come home when he woke up next morning. But when he suggested that he go with her (and feigned interest), she smiled kindly and said he didn't have to do that for her, she knew he didn't enjoy that sort of noise and hoopla anymore; besides, these were girls' nights, and he didn't really fit into the group. Anger welled up in him, but he kept it hidden. He felt as if he were waking up from a dream and facing cold reality. When they were first getting to know each other, he always thought she was too pretty and lively to spare a second glance for a wet blanket like him. He always chickened out of flirting with her. In the end it was she who wound up pursuing him. By then she had met his gaze many times, but he'd always looked away in fright. The first night they slept together, she said: 'It's about time I got to know a good boy.' It had seemed too good to be true, and now that appeared to be the case after all.

He had made it west of the roundabout on Hringbraut. He thought to himself that he would have to head home now, but turned into the Melar neighbourhood and enjoyed driving slowly through near-empty streets for a while.

R.E.M.'s 'Losing My Religion' was playing on the radio. They were still playing this song that had become so popular last year. His English wasn't as good as he would have liked, but the lyrics seemed to be about a man who had lost his faith. Something like that. It was a beautiful song, but sad, and it awakened feelings of melancholy and sorrow in him. When the guitar played its saddest tune, the lyrics were '... That was just a dream ... that was just a dream.'

'I need to pee,' said the boy in the back seat at the very moment when the car lumbered past the University Theatre. Twenty-one years earlier, the man himself had said those same words to the delivery truck driver in this exact same place. He had no recollection if it, and nobody knew of this coincidence. He knew there was a shop a few hundred metres further south, but didn't remember that it had been an RCGR shop. He drove there.

There wasn't much going on at the shop, and he managed to speak to a girl at the register who showed them down into the basement. The toilet was in the same place as before, but the actual toilet bowl and sink had been replaced since the summer of 1970. A clip-on lampshade encased two light bulbs in place of the bare, dangling one. The walls were white now, not red.

The man had no idea that he had been in this toilet before. But on the edge of the sink was a shaving kit: a razor, a bottle of foam, and a container of Gillette aftershave. Obviously one of the employees preferred to shave at work rather than at home. It reminded him of something old; he couldn't recall what.

When he pulled the boy's trousers up, he noticed that his underpants were damp. The boy must have had a bit of an accident in the car. He slipped them off, pulled some paper towels out of a metal box (which had not been there in the summer of 1970) on the wall, wet them and washed the boy's crotch, then dried it with another towel. The trousers were dry, and he put them on the boy again, rinsed the underpants in the sink and wrung them. He felt a moment of pure happiness, enjoyed taking care of the boy. The boy was silent and appeared neither happy nor sad. The man picked him up in his arms and looked at them both in the mirror, tried to see a resemblance, whether a coincidental one or one that had mysteriously developed because of the time they spent together. He could feel the boy's body and imagined his familiar silhouette. They had drastically different builds; the boy was slender and long-legged, tall for his age, while he himself would always be pegged as a little bit fat even though he wasn't overweight, because he was short, had a protruding neck, and was slow in his movements. The boy got his gangly build from his father, who was a regular at the pub. They had long since broken up when he met her, but they interacted at the pub like old friends. Once he had seen them share a deep kiss that nevertheless was somehow meaningless, like a show. That same evening she took a seat next to where he himself was sitting, and they slept together that night.

The boy was quiet, but his father was loud and verbose. He often slapped men on the back and sometimes yelled at them for no apparent to shut the hell up, but then burst out laughing within moments. He could be threatening in his merriment. Tall and gangly, often wearing a short leather jacket. He could give the impression of being a self-educated expert in disability and accident benefits. He had been in a motorcycle crash and two car accidents, though you wouldn't know to look at him. For this reason he was unable to work, but all the same it seemed to be a full-time job for him, a challenging and complex one, to demand his rights. He was constantly detailing the assessments of this or that doctor, his communications with insurance companies and the Social Insurance Administration. In between stories he cracked jokes, and a mischievous, teasing gleam appeared in his eyes that caused many of those around him to keep their heads down.

Friday traffic was at its peak, and long trains of cars stretched along every lane on Miklabraut, inching along at walking pace; to make matters worse, there had been a collision at the front of the queue, out of sight. But he wasn't in a rush, and he was quite content to be carried along slowly by this stream; felt like part of a whole. Which led his mind back to the fact that he had just been promoted; he was a man who enjoyed people's trust.

He stopped the car at a traffic light and didn't make the next one, the traffic was so heavy. That was all right. Next to him was a woman in a very old BMW. She herself was well dressed and didn't seem poor despite the rust spots on the car. She was an attractive woman, probably in her mid-thirties. She was alone in the car. He looked at her for a long time without her noticing. He wasn't in the habit of looking at women, not since he himself started cohabiting, and it wasn't beauty that caught his attention in this case, but rather something else: she looked worried, so worried that the sight of her was searing, her face all silent anguish. As soon as the traffic thinned, she vanished from sight. Her visage immediately shattered in his mind and left behind only a faceless anguish that reminded him of the enduring fact of his own worries. He had grown so used to feeling anxious that sometimes he forgot the specific cause of his concerns for hours. At times he felt as though his worries didn't actually exist, but meanwhile they would continue to churn beneath the surface of his mind ready to burst forth at any moment.

He knew she would go out this weekend. Maybe he would lie awake and hear her come home at 2 or 3 am; then he would pretend to be asleep so she wouldn't think he was suspicious enough to stay up for her. Maybe he would sleep through her arrival and wake up with no clue of when she had turned up. He wouldn't ask, after all. He sometimes thought that if his life were a story in a book or a TV show they would be constantly at each other's throats about her

112

weekend revelry. But life was different; there was more silence in it.

His eyes fell on a clear plastic bag containing the boy's urine-soaked underpants, lying on the car floor. He had got the plastic bag in the sweet shop. During the first months of their living together, the boy had still been in diapers. He hadn't tried to avoid diaper duty, quite the contrary. When he did it he felt like the boy was his own. They had both been his at that time; they had been his family. Now there was more uncertainty in his soul on that point, though he tried to tell himself that nothing had changed.

He walked ahead of the boy from the parking lot to the stairwell. Then he thought of the child behind him and saw himself, a small boy, walk behind a man in a plaid shirt; they had both just stepped out of a delivery van... He couldn't remember more.

He stopped, turned around, and waited for the boy with an outstretched hand. The boy took it and they walked silently into the apartment building, hand in hand.

The woman was sick with the flu. She had curled up on the living room sofa under the duvet, an old scarf of his around her neck. It was a black, thin scarf that he hadn't seen for a long time and had completely forgotten about. It gladdened him to see the scarf around her neck, a useless garment that he had acquired before he knew she existed, an artefact of singlehood.

She asked whether there was something decent on TV tonight. On the screen was the film he had been watching alone last Friday; he kept recording the films she missed while she was out partying even though she had long since stopped asking him to. Now it had come in handy. The image was frozen, the tape paused. On the screen was a man in a tight, plaid jacket and a bright green shirt. He seemed grotesque, his clothing tasteless and his too-thick hair sticking up into the air. Last Friday he had solved a murder mystery and spared a helpful innocent from a bit of unpleasant knowledge. On that occasion he hadn't noticed anything grotesque about the man. But everything somehow became more flawed and worthy of criticism when she was around, and he involuntarily felt as though this film character's appearance were his responsibility.

He asked about her illness, tried to seem concerned and hide how relieved he was, but maybe he tried too hard, because she seemed to see straight through him and grinned. Then she touched his arm and asked him whether he could cook dinner. He accepted gladly and tried to ignore the look of pity on her face. He started by looking up the TV listings in the newspaper he had pinched from the mailbox downstairs, but then the boy called for him from his bedroom: 'Daddydaddy, I got the tow truck to pick up the police car!' *Daddy!* Yes, of course the boy calls him Daddy. Suddenly he felt like reality was just a journey from one dream to the next. Now he was waking from a bad dream to a good one: the woman safely ensconced in the living room and the boy calling him Daddy. And he about to cook dinner for all three of them. This was authentic family life.

He went into the child's room. The boy had hooked the crane of a yellow tow truck under the fender of a blue police car. His father had given him the tow truck, but he himself had given him the police car. Suddenly the boy swung the tow truck around with both hands, slinging the police car into the wall, and let out a loud explosion noise for emphasis.

It occurred to him that this was a rather immature way to play, even though the boy was only four years old. But he had no way of gauging that, really.

He went into the kitchen. There was minced meat in the freezer that he could defrost in the microwave. There was also a ready-made casserole in a package, and even garlic bread.

He stepped into the toilet to wash his hands before cooking. He was surprised to see in the mirror how red his face was. His thick cheeks were bright red and his eyes bloodshot. It was as if he didn't know how he felt, as if he were gripped with strong emotions even though he believed he was calm. He asked himself whether he were embarrassed, angry, or just strung out. The woman's piteous glance from just a moment ago resurfaced in his mind. But he felt only calm, and the flush gradually receded from his face.

He felt as though he were on an island, as if this evening were an island in the ocean of time. Past and future didn't matter. Nothing mattered but the moment, and he was safe in it. Suddenly he remembered the bag with the boy's soiled underwear out in the car. He had forgotten to bring it inside. Some day this bag would be an ancient memory, or rather it would get buried in a sea of forgotten details. Where would he be then? He had lived 29 years and 10 months. He had lived with his mother in the West End, among those old grey and brown stone houses, with trees in the yards and quiet streets that he had just been driving through; he had lived alone in rented rooms here and there in the city, worked in a construction supply store and a paint factory and finally at a petrol station, sometimes walked to work with the scarf around his neck, the one the woman was now wearing in the living room. None of this mattered now, and the times they were living now wouldn't matter at all later on. Suddenly he felt that it was completely pointless to worry about anything at all.

He looked at the sink. Thought about the toilet in the sweet shop earlier and the shaving kit by the sink. He saw his mother hold a steel-grey jug of coffee and say: 'Won't you sit a moment longer? Shall I make crèpes?' There was a smell of cologne, a plaid shirt, hairy arms. The memory was lonely.

In his mind, shiny, bright red walls appeared. He had no idea where they were from, but they seemed familiar. He turned on the tap and the red walls vanished from his mind as though the water had washed them away.

Disappearing into the World

1975

THOUGH MY BROTHER'S illness dominated our family life, he takes up even more space since he died. Sometimes I wonder whether I'll ever be rid of him.

The living room is not large, and now there is no space in it for anything but him. Before he just took up the floor. He built a farm in one corner: a brown plastic fence, cows, sheep and dogs; and the farmer cut the rug with a scythe that was attached to his hands. In the other corner he built a city of Lego blocks, and the city kept growing and stretching farther out onto the floor, like the new houses in the neighbourhood that keep popping up and growing closer and closer. Sometimes the farmer had to go to the city in a car that had been built there, and at such times it was impossible to plant a foot anywhere on the entire floor.

Now his toys are nowhere to be seen, but on top of the living room cabinet sits a row of photographs of him in leather frames propped up on legs. On the centre of the cabinet shelf stands the green memorial vase from the hospital. In the morning I am sometimes jolted awake from a dream of playing ball in the living room, just as the ball crashes into the vase.

Two large pictures of him hang on the wall. One is a photograph with a dark green, painted background. His

117

cheeks are swollen with oedema, but his visage is bright and radiant. His expression is serious, and there is a hint of accusation in his eyes.

The other picture is a portrait, another memorial gift from the hospital. The face in that picture is not a very good likeness, but the shirt is familiar: multicoloured stripes in the style of the Beatles. We both had shirts like that, but they've been cut up into dusting cloths long since. The other day I saw Mum wipe the picture down with a piece of one of the shirts. I hope it was my shirt, though it doesn't matter.

Every day I have to go to the cemetery with Mum. These can end up being long walks, because not only is Mum interested in my brother's grave, she wants to educate me about the lives of a number of other denizens of the graveyard.

Mostly, though, she talks about what she wants to do to my brother's grave. In the space of one year she's replaced the tombstone three times, each one more spectacular than the last.

Sometimes Mum seems particularly affectionate towards me when I walk with her in the cemetery. 'You're sure to become a doctor,' she says and looks at me lovingly. 'You'll be a doctor and save lives.' I think with a shudder about spending my adulthood in a hospital wearing a white coat. I've always imagined that as an adult I would finally be free. Could spend my days making gory movies and sit at a custom-made card table at night, sipping whisky from a glass that slips into a round slot on the table when I set it down.

But when Mum says this and looks at me so affectionately, the medical career seems unavoidable. For a long time I want nothing so much as to become a doctor. In a fiery passion I write an essay about it in school. Regret soon follows, but I ignore it.

Instead of getting rid of one brother I've had two foisted upon me. One of them lies in the cemetery, but the other one Mum talks about at the breakfast table: 'You know your brother is still alive. Not only that: now he's not sick anymore. He lives in another dimension and watches us. He sees us even though we can't see him. But because you're a sensitive boy, maybe you'll be able to see him sometime, or at least hear him. You want that, don't you?'

Mum takes silence as consent and continues: 'When you're alone up here, you can sit in the living room and do something. It's a method that sensitive people can use. You let your arms lie on the armrests of the chair and your open palms face upward. You close your eyes and try not to think about anything. Empty your mind. Then you never know, you might hear him. If you hear him you should open your eyes, and maybe you'll *see* him too!'

Mum places a brown notebook and a blue Bic pen on the kitchen table. The notebook looks exactly like the ones I use at school, but this one is empty. And this book I don't have to keep in my schoolbag and I don't have to do homework in it. This book I don't have to use any more than I want to; Mum emphasises that as she looks at me with pleading eyes.

It's actually not me who is supposed to write in the book. She shows me how to use the pen; it's supposed to rest in the crease between index finger and thumb. The point of the pen at the top of the page. The hand motionless.

If he writes something, Mum wants to see it. But she repeats that I don't have to do this any more than I want to. The pleading eyes. I sense that I need to be rid of these pleading eyes at once. I feel that they're worse than any amount of scolding, though I can hardly compare the two, since I'm never scolded about anything.

Mum is content with just a single little sentence. She's thrilled, to tell the truth. The handwriting is quite unclear, but the words 'perfectly healthy' can be clearly deciphered from the chicken scratch at the end of the line. Mum infers that the sentence in the notebook is the same as the one I tell her I heard in the living room: 'Don't be sad, I feel well, I'm perfectly healthy.'

'Are you sure he didn't say anything else to you?' she asks eagerly.

'No, and I got the feeling that maybe he didn't want to be spoken to any more. As if he should just live his life over there in the other dimension. And we should live ours.'

A confused, questioning look on Mum's face.

'Did he *say* that?'

'No no, I just got that impression somehow. Maybe because I'm kind of a sensitive boy like you said.'

She asks whether I won't try again anyway.

I say I'll wait and see. You need to sense whether you should try again. Because you're kind of sensitive to these things.

Mum says maybe I want to be a medium when I grow up. A medium and a doctor. In the world there are both good doctors and good mediums, but she doesn't know of anyone who is both.

'Such a man would be a great blessing for mankind.'

I nod and swallow saliva.

When I walk into the empty living room, nothing seems more natural than for my brother's face on the big photo on the wall to start talking.

But when I lay my arms on the armrests, open my palms, close my eyes and try to empty my mind, the traffic outside suddenly becomes so loud that the car noises that you usually don't notice sound like I'm standing on the street.

Then you sense how large and noisy the world is; the silence is just here. Full of mortal life, the world awaits beyond the din of traffic that disappears into the distance.

1976

Sometimes I feel like I have to make it to the cinema every day. But that's out of the question. In my bed at night I make my own films. Red bullet holes burst forth on the suits, and men writhe in front of me. One after another they try to die as spectacularly as possible for me, sink shaking to the floor with as much style as they can muster.

That isn't death.

On my nightstand is tap-water whisky in a glass. After the bloodbath, I sit up in bed and empty the glass in a single gulp. I frown and let out a breath; the liquid burns in my innards.

I'm never stopped at 14-and-over films, but when the films are 16-and-over it's hit or miss. It's no fun to go back home with a ticket in your pocket that, by theatre rules, can't be refunded. But I certainly feel like the criminals on the silver screen when I try to maintain a low profile at the entrance as I proffer the ticket. By the time the doorman rips the stub off I've made my escape into the aircraft that will take me out of the jurisdiction, while the cops who've dispersed through the airport come away empty-handed. They can't stop me. They can't stop my revenge. I will find my brother's killer.

Our grocery shop is on the ground floor of the house. It's a little shop, but Mum always calls it The Grocery Shop. She says it with pride, and in title case: The Grocery Shop. The product shelves are in a little doorless room next to the entrance. The cash register in a cramped corner just inside. On the table is a grey phone that I once thought very modern. Before it was bought I thought all phones were black. But now this grey phone seems just as commonplace as the dust on the floor, while the black phone in the living room reminds me of an old half-forgotten time: when my brother wasn't sick and I could play with him and tease him like a normal kid.

The storeroom is in a heated shed in the back yard. There

I strike up a friendship with forgotten ice cream sauces. They stand in clear plastic bottles with red caps in a straight line behind a box stuffed chock-full of lightbulbs.

The lightbulbs are covered with a thick layer of dust that I sometimes draw a line in with my index finger. Without fail, I find that on every return visit to the shed, the evidence is gone, the layer of dust as thick as before. It makes me feel as though I can't make any impact on the world.

The bottles of ice cream sauce are tinted in different colours by their contents. Just before I squirt the contents of one into my mouth I feel a joyous sensation that is quite the opposite of the emptiness evoked by the lightbulb dust: *I* and only *I* dictate how much is in the sauce bottles at any given moment.

But a short while later, when I've begun feeling sick, the emptiness returns: the bottles are forgotten and abandoned, and affecting them makes no impact on the world. The bottles are nothing but a part of myself, like my socks or a face I make in the mirror in private.

An expiration date has been stamped on the label on the front of each bottle. Though you can't tell by tasting them, the stamps show that all of the sauces expired in February 1974. My brother was still alive then. I wonder what he looks like now, how long the body lasts.

1977

When I'm finally rid of my brother I entangle myself in his net again. Now he isn't the topic of conversation anymore; I don't have to think about him.

I've lived long enough to be considered a teenager, but has anything changed? I had always imagined that, as soon as I became a teenager, coolness would automatically descend upon me, a leather jacket would fall from the sky upon my shoulders and a flying cigarette emplace itself in the corner of my mouth, see-sawing there in an even rhythm while I fired off razor-sharp repartee.

But I don't dare to smoke, and I who have so often drunk fake whisky from the kitchen tap and swallowed it with carefully rehearsed grimaces and sighs à la the tough guys from the movies - in reality, I shrink away from a real mixed vodka drink.

The only thing that's changed is that now I'm never turned away from restricted films. There's nothing remarkable about getting into a 16-and-over film at the age of 15. The boys who once listened to me with rapt attention after I had snuck in to see *Deliverance* at the theatre in the East End were now waving booze in my face.

'C'mon, aren't you gonna have some? Scared of your mummy?'

'Nah, I just prefer whisky.'

It's still irresistible to sit in a darkened room where death is entertaining, exciting and worry-free. No drawn-out funeral, no loaded silence in the house, no trips to the cemetery, no brown notebook that now lies forgotten in the bottom drawer in the kitchen among batteries and screwdrivers, underneath cutlery and wooden spoons.

It used to be easy to pinch a few bills from the cash register, but Mum has sold the shop now. I can't quite make out exactly what she sold, though, because we still live in the house and the storage shed still stands on the back lot, with goods inside.

My brother used to collect ten-krónur coins in a canvas bag that Mum gave him after getting change from the bank. The bag filled up slowly but surely. My brother found a tenner under a sofa cushion, in the driveway, on the floor, and so on. People gave him tenners; I even gave him one once.

He was imitating Scrooge McDuck's fortune from the

Disney magazine. There were bags like these in the pictures. To perfect the imitation he drew a dollar sign on the bag with a black marker. Now there's only a faint mark from the pen, and I don't know whether my eyes can still discern the real dollar sign or whether it's my memory that reads it.

It takes me a long time to count all the tenners from the bag. All told they're worth slightly more than a cinema ticket, a bag of popcorn, and two bus fares.

The bottles of ice cream sauce have vanished from the shed. And the box of bulbs, too. Now I feel like my brother's spirit lived in this stuff, and I'm glad to be rid of it. On the floor stands an open Cheerios carton, half-full of yellow packages. A few cartons of Viceroy cigarettes lie on a wooden table. The heating has been shut off in the shed, and it's a strange feeling after all these warm years to be cold all of a sudden, standing here in a t-shirt.

Mum has bought a dry-cleaning shop in the East End. It's hard to sneak into the register. The steam from the garment press has a funny smell to it. It's fun to breathe in for a few days, but then it becomes commonplace.

The film is a disappointment; more of a comedy than an action movie despite the age limit. There was only one murder in the whole film, even though the ticket price had been upped. I felt cheated, as I had paid a hundred krónur less for my last cinema ticket and seen at least seven murders. All the same, I couldn't deny myself the popcorn. Now I can't afford the bus and have to walk home.

On the way home I realise that summer has begun to fade away. A chill breeze and pale blue twilight. As if I were coming home from a nine o'clock screening and not a seven o'clock.

The empty bag of tenners becomes a knot in my stomach. The jewel thieves in the film, and their audacity, come to mind. For a brief moment I feel like I'm worse than they are. I feel that they haven't stolen anything that matters. And it's a minor detail that they shot and killed a security guard. I envision him drinking coffee in the actors' cafeteria, with the fake bloodstain still on the front of his shirt.

I wonder whether I could want to be a doctor again.

1978

I got accepted into the secondary school today. Mum was thrilled, and even though we knew all the kids in this neighbourhood got into this school once they finished their elementary diploma, we felt victorious. We celebrated at a restaurant: chicken, fries, and pilsner. Mum told me that two of my close cousins had received their secondary diplomas from this school. Both had died in accidents.

'Now you will pick up their banner,' she said, eyes shining.

But she didn't say a single word about medicine. In my mind's eye I saw a student cap on my head, and imagined being mistaken for a police officer.

I took a sip of the pilsner and imagined it was stronger, was about to grimace but decided against it. I thought about the letter from the secondary school and decided I'd outgrown that.

At the next table, an old man gnawed on a chicken bone. I had often seen this man in our shop at home back in the old days, but he didn't seem to recognise us anymore, even though I met his eyes. Mum didn't notice him.

For a brief moment, everything became dull again, like when a cloud suddenly blocks the sun and you're still wearing shorts.

On the way home, Mum stopped the car in front of the secondary school building and looked at it for a long time. A red Skoda honked behind us, but Mum couldn't care less.

The old shop cash register is still on the desk. It doesn't seem to have gone with the sale last year, any more than most of the other stuff. The black power cord coils itself up beside it. I manage to open the money drawer, but I can't close it again. The drawer is empty. For some reason it doesn't occur to me to plug the cord in.

I take a seat in the living room. The pictures of my brother on the wall aren't stifling anymore. Once you couldn't watch TV without their interrupting and saying with their silence that you should do something else, suffer and adopt a holy expression. Now they've become old things, and old things have no life unless you make an effort to keep their flame alive.

That's what time is like: you don't notice it passing until it has passed. Nothing seems to happen day-by-day; you don't notice change until you realise that everything has changed.

I think of how when Mum and I drove away to the restaurant tonight, the sound of the car must have carried into the living room, grown distant, and then disappeared, just like other car sounds – if someone had been at home to listen. And before long I can't stave off the feeling that I myself was here in the room, that I listened to myself disappear into the world and become unrecognisable.

About the Author

Ágúst Borgþór Sverrisson has published five collections of short stories – *Twice in a Lifetime* being his latest – plus a short-novel, *Hliðarspor* (Sidestep) in 2007. He is widely regarded as one of Iceland's most accomplished practitioners of the short form. His stories have been translated into English and German, and two of those featured in this collection, 'Disappearing into the World' and 'The First Day of the Fourth Week', are high-school set texts in his home country. 'Disappearing into the World' won the Strik.is prize in 2001. Agust has worked as a journalist, copywriter and translator and is a well-known blogger and commentator in Iceland on literature and politics.

About the Translators

María Helga Guðmundsdóttir, a translator of English, Icelandic, and German, holds degrees in German literature and geology from Stanford University, where her thesis was awarded the Golden Medal for Excellence in the Humanities and Creative Arts. Her most recent translation is *The Eskimo Lady: Biography of an Icelandic Dwarf in America* by Inga Dóra Björnsdóttir.

Anna Benassi is certified by the Icelandic Ministry of Justice as a translator of Icelandic and English. She holds a bachelor's degree from Manhattan School of Music. Her previous literary translations include *Benjamin Dove* by Fridrik Erlingsson, *The Egg* by Áslaug Jónsdóttir, and Björk Jakobsdóttir's play *Cellophane*.

Vera Júlíusdóttir is an Icelandic translator and filmmaker. Her translations include *History of Film* by David Parkinson, English translations for the Icelandic website www.literature. is, and the short story 'The Water People' ('Vatnsfólkið') by Gyrðir Elíasson, winner of the Nordic Council Literature Prize 2011, which appears in *Elsewhere: Short Stories from Small Town Europe* (Comma, 2007). Vera lives and works in London.

ALSO AVAILABLE FROM COMMA TRANSLATION:

Stone Tree

Gyrðir Elíasson

Translated from the Icelandic by Victoria Cribb

ISBN 9781905583089
RRP: £7.99

** *Winner of the 2011 Nordic Council Literature Prize* **

Gyrðir Elíasson's stories take us out of ourselves. Situated on the lonely western shores of Iceland, or out in the vast mountain ranges or barren lava fields of this spectacular country, each one is a study in self-exile. We follow a Boston ornithologist, speeding through the landscape in a four-by-four, chasing Arctic Terns; a schoolboy relocating to the northernmost town of Siglufjördur to compete in a chess tournament; a husband packing his wife off to visit her aunt in Sweden. In almost every story we find people taking leave of their normal lives in order to take their dreams more seriously.

Praise for *Stone Tree*:

'In vivid and haunting prose, Eliasson shows how no man can be an island, as community intrudes upon their self-exile in the most unexpected ways.'
- The Independent on Sunday

www.commapress.co.uk